Lost Myself for a Minute

Lost Myself
for a Minute

Michael Burnett

Published by Annecy Press LLC
Zion. Il 60099
Annecypress.com

First paperback edition May 2023

Cover photo taken by the author
Author photo (on back cover): courtesy of Kelly Trapp
Author photo (interior): taken by a pilgrim at San Anton
Copyeditors: Kristin Davis, Paige Lawson, and Shaun Baines
Book Cover design: Onur Burc

ISBN 978-1-7378175-2-9 (paperback)
ISBN 978-1-7378175-3-6 (ebook)
LIBRARY OF CONGRESS CONTROL NUMBER: 2023906636

Publisher's Cataloging-in-Publication data

Names: Burnett, Michael, author.
Title: Lost myself for a minute / Michael Burnett.
Description: Zion, IL: Annecy Press, 2023.
Identifiers: LCCN: | ISBN: 978-1-7378175-2-9 (paperback) | 978-1-7378175-3-6 (ebook)
Subjects: LCSH Strada di Francia (Italy and France)--Fiction. | Camino de Santiago de Compostela--Fiction. | Love stories. | Bildungsroman. | BISAC FICTION / Coming of Age
Classification: LCC PS3603 .U87 L67 2023 | DDC 813.6--dc23

Printed in the United States of America

To my mom and Christy –

Thank you for all your love and support.

The only person you are destined to become is the person you decide to be.

—Ralph Waldo Emerson

ONE / dark

June 18 –   Dekalb, Illinois

I pull into a parking space just outside our apartment door, for the last time. The sun reflects off the hood and into my eyes Eminem's *Walk on Water* stops abruptly.

Brody and I get out and walk around to the back of the car.

"That was epic, bro," he says, with his cheesy grin.

"I can't believe half of what we did," I say, smiling. "I'm glad you decided to come along."

Then, a few seconds later, I say, "These are gonna make for some great memories someday."

"Yeah," he says, still smiling, "yeah, they will. That was one hell of a last hurrah."

He puts his hands on my shoulders, and with his brows raised, looks me in the eyes and says in a serious tone, "Good luck with everything." Then nodding, adds, "And Jack, if you need anything, call me."

"You too," I say, then add, "Shit, you're gonna be working in a few days. I feel for *you*." I smirk.

"I know. It all starts now … real life."

"For you, yeah," I say. "But I'm still in limbo."

We share a long, tight hug, ending with pats on each other's backs.

He grabs his backpack which leaves only my two large duffel bags in the trunk. I lower the hatch.

I get in the car and, as I'm backing up, I say out the window, "I'll keep in touch."

As I pull away, from the rearview, I see Brody waving his farewell as Eminem continues his rant. I widen my eyes to keep from tearing up; I have difficulty swallowing. I'm going to miss him, and my life here.

I just dropped off my best friend from college at our soon to be old apartment. We just returned from a three-week road trip to California, and points in between. It was full of outdoor adventures; days in the wild hiking through canyons, climbing mountains, and swimming in ice-cold lakes. We had some wild adventures in cities, too.

As I drive through campus, I pass the dorm I lived in freshman year. It is there, where I met those who I'd end up spending most of my time with the last two years. I stop at the convenience store where I know my fake I.D. will work. I fill an extra-large Styrofoam cup with ice and grab two cans of Wicked Cider from the cooler. Sitting in my car, I empty both into my cup, then toss the empty cans in the garbage as I roll past. This well-practiced routine is my secret.

My sadness remains as I leave this town that has been my home. I think about the fact that nearly everything I own is in these two duffels. It feels good in a way, the freedom, but I also wish I had deeper roots.

Brody just graduated from Northern.

I just flunked out.

He landed a good job in Denver.

While I … have no idea.

I head north, toward Madison, Wisconsin, to visit Jimmy, my best friend from high school. I sip my drink and think about tonight. I'm excited to finally see the U.W. campus and am stoked for a night out. I feel bad I haven't been up to see him the last two years. Last year, he took the *bus* to see me. It would have been much easier for me, with my car. My car; when my mom bought it for me junior year, she said, "You better take care of it, you're not getting another." And I have.

The drive north is easy. It's just a hundred miles straight up I-90. I cross the border and the scenery changes, from farmers' fields to rolling hills of green. I think about my life, really dwell, uncertain where to go from here.

This visit to Madison is my way of putting off going to see my mom and brothers. I haven't told her about failing out. She has no clue. I didn't even tell her I was going out West.

I feel like a loser, failing at something I know I could do. I know my mom is going to be disappointed in me. So will my dad.

A question I always ask. "And dad?"

The scenes of *that* day flash in my head, despite my efforts to forget. A painful memory that I'll do almost anything to avoid.

I drive too fast and think about what to do with my life.

Get a real job, nine-to-five … but then I'd be stuck.

Go to community college … and study what.

Once home, I fear my bad habits will return. Booze and drugs with a group I'd escaped, but going back, the temptation remains.

My days will be empty … fuck.

Vanlife is something I've considered. Living out of a cheap van, or even my car … travelling around with a dog. It's not like I have close friends around anyway. It wouldn't be a bad life; too bad money's a thing. I have some saved, but it's not enough to last.

While I'm at a loss for my next step, I feel worse for my mom. She's always supported me, in every way she could; even spoiling me, if I'm honest. My failing out of school is clearly on me, but, knowing her, she'll take responsibility, thinking it was something *she* did wrong raising me. I know that's not true. She is hardworking, always doing her best. She's raising three boys alone, which, sometimes, I'm sure, has her feeling overwhelmed.

My failure … I don't want her to *feel* that. I don't want her to *see* that, every day.

But right now, it's my only option.

Ideally, I'd be going back to school in the fall. My college days were a blast. Away from home for the first time; I loved hanging with my volleyball crew, our passion shared; exploring myself in altered states and, of course, the girls. It was the best time of my life.

But my laziness ruined it. That was the *only* thing. A couple of friends are transferring, but I'm the only one who failed out; everyone else not graduating will be back. I'll miss all the fun times I could have had.

What I need to do while I'm in Madison, is come up with a plan; something to tell my mom. I've tried to think up something before, but my mind just wanders. Maybe a deadline will help … I have until Sunday night. If I can't, I'll need to make one up as I go along, and I'm afraid where that might lead.

I find a spot in the suggested lot and use Google to find his place.

Walking … it *feels* great after being cooped up in a car for the last thirty-six hours straight. My head dances as *Uptown Funk* plays on repeat through Air Pods; my buzz near its peak.

The weather is perfect; sunny and seventy-five degrees. The time, half past seven. I'm in a t-shirt, shorts, and sandals.

Jimmy opens the door, a smile on his clean-shaven face.

We hug.

"It's great to see you, Jack."

"You too," I say, my smile affixed.

I walk in. It's immaculate. No surprise there. He has framed pictures on the wall, a couch, a table, and four chairs.

"So, what are you up for tonight? I know you've been driving for days."

"I'm good. I'd love to hit a bar or two."

"Yeah. If that's what you want. I'm sure it'll be fun."

I drop my bag and we head straight out. A couple of hours later, we are sitting in a bar. Jimmy nurses his first beer, while I'm on my third. He never was much of a drinker. We trade stories of our high school days; cruising around in my car, going on double dates, getting sick after chewing his dad's tobacco. These times I look back on and smile. He had been my best friend since the first grade, living just across the alley. As we got older, he was the only friend who stayed sober.

I tell him about my recent road trip.

He talks of home and school.

Eventually, he says, "I've got an early class."

I respond, "Okay, just one more."

Thirty minutes later, we're on our way back to his apartment. There's been no deep conversation, mostly me sharing stories of my drunken escapades. Then Jimmy starts to speak, "I hope...", he hesitates, then says, "I hope you can get things figured out. If not for you, at least for your mom's sake."

I feel hurt.

"Don't worry. I will," I say, a little too aggressively.

"You haven't been home to see your family since Christmas. How do you think that makes your mom feel?"

"I don't have to explain myself."

"You don't, but you should to your mom," he says. "And, why you wasted the last two years."

I remain silent.

"You have a good heart, Jack. I've seen it. But you just can't keep running—and you should watch your drinking."

"I'm not running," I snap. "And, I have cut back." I lie.

"Okay ... It's just that I'm worried about you," he says as he reaches out and touches my shoulder.

I look down. "You don't need to worry."

"If I can do anything, just let me know."

"There is nothing you can do. It's me. I've got to figure it out."

"Make sure you do."

He gets off the couch and points to a closet. "There are pillows and blankets in there. Sleep well."

"Good night," I say, my head still hanging down, my eyes closed.

I appreciate that he's always been there for me; but his perfection is sometimes hard to take. I don't feel jealous, as I don't want to be like him, but I struggle when it's obvious that I don't measure up.

After his bedroom door closes, I get up and walk to the fridge. Inside, a six-pack of Coors Light, my favorite.

TWO / light

June 19 –   Madison, Wisconsin

I wake to a slight throbbing in my head. I open my eyes; dry, my contacts are still in, and see Jimmy's pack is gone. I look around for a clock but don't see one, so I dig out my iPhone. It's already after nine. I roll off the couch and find a note on the coffee table.

"Jack - I have classes all day. I'll be back around four. Have fun on campus."

My stomach starts to churn, and it's not from my drinking. I've messed up again. My head starts to throb harder.

After last night, I don't want to spend the next two nights here. Despite not wanting to go home, I'm leaving, but only after I explore the campus. I take a piss, brush my teeth, and write a response on the back of Jimmy's note.

"I'm gonna head out. I'm sorry about last night."

I know I was in the wrong, but I still didn't like being called out on my shit.

I grab my things and go. I walk down a residential street, passing others my age who are out walking dogs, or wearing backpacks, probably headed to work or a summer class. I think to myself that most I pass are being productive, while I am only killing time.

The sun is already high in the sky. I'm in the same clothes from last night. I head toward the main buildings on campus and think about what I should do. Maybe I'll take another road trip for a few days, head up north, hike, and sleep in my car. I shake my head and laugh when I think of it as practice for Vanlife.

The idea of living for months in my car, wandering around the West, seems the best option, given I still have money in the bank. The handful of credits I earned in the last two years, obviously were not worth the money spent. Running away from failure, and I know that's what it is, seems like the least painful option right now.

The U.W. campus is expansive and sits on a rise, or at least part of it does. I look down to a large lake; well-manicured with lush green spaces scattered about. I pass regal looking buildings, mostly dorms it seems, and then more modern ones as I move away from the lake. Students, like me in shorts and t-shirts, are lying on the open greens, most with cell phones in hand.

As I roam the streets, I google "coffee shop" before heading to my car. I decide on Colectivo Coffee, about a twenty-minute walk. On the way, I pass my green Subaru Outback, still covered in dirt from the Utah desert.

"Jack," the barista calls out.

I grab my Americano and croissant and find a seat next to an open window, really a garage door, next to the sidewalk.

I sip my coffee, watching the passersby, wondering what my mom will say, or more accurately, think. I haven't told her about what's been happening. I texted her before finals week saying I was going to hang around campus for a while.

An elderly but energetic woman walks past and flashes me a wide smile. I smile back. She's an attractive woman with short gray hair and a deep tan. She is carrying a Madison Public Library book bag on her shoulder. She walks into the coffee shop, takes a bright yellow flyer out of her bag, pins it to the community board, then leaves. As she walks by again, our eyes meet and hold for a beat, another smile which turns into a chuckle.

My curiosity piqued, I walk over to see what she left.

The sign reads, *I am looking for a student available for light maintenance and upkeep on a large home in exchange for room and board. If interested, Call Lily,* her phone number is given.

In a split second, I decide. I want to talk to her. I grab my pack, toss my coffee cup, and head in her direction. I start to sweat as I get closer, unsure what to say, but something happened when I read her sign. I envisioned myself living in Madison. Why? I have no idea.

I pull up alongside her and immediately say, "Excuse me."

She turns towards me, recognizes me, and smiles. She slows her pace then stops and looks behind her as if she dropped something.

"Are you Lily?"

"Indeed, I am."

"I'm Jack," I say. "I just saw your flyer."

"Are you interested?" She seems surprised.

"Yes," I say, hesitating, then add, "but, I'm not a student here."

"That's okay," she says in a soothing voice, "I put student, since that is who I assumed, might be interested."

"Great!"

"Are you up for a walk?"

"Sure," I respond with a nod.

"I live 1.3 miles from Colectivo. We can talk while we walk."

"Perfect," I say with a grin.

We resume walking, side by side.

"So, what is it you do if you are not going to school?"

"I'm just moving to the area," I lie.

"Did you go to school before?"

"Yeah, I did," I say, trying my best to be respectful. "I went to Northern Illinois, but I didn't do so hot."

"Looking for a fresh start?"

"You can say that," I say, nodding.

"That's understandable."

"What sort of things do you need done around your house?"

She hesitates for a few seconds, then says, "Some painting … and I'd like another raised garden bed … a handful of other odds and ends, but nothing too hard."

"I can handle that," I say confidently, "and anything else you might need."

Lily's gait is smooth. She glides next to me as we head in the direction of campus, our pace brisk.

"When did you stop taking classes at N.I.U.?"

"I finished the spring semester."

"What have you been doing since finals?"

"My best friend and I just got back from a road trip … yesterday, actually."

"Where did you go?"

"We drove to California."

"It sounds like quite the adventure," she says, as she looks over and makes eye contact.

"It was," I say with a smile.

"My husband and I traveled often. We loved Wyoming, especially the Tetons."

"Me too!" I say excitedly. "My friend, Brody, and I just backpacked up Cascade Canyon to a mountain lake."

"Charles and I have hiked there several times over the years," she says. "He passed away two years ago."

"I'm sorry."

"Thank you," she says. Her melancholic smile remains for a second, then she asks, "Where is your hometown?"

"A small town in Illinois, Zion. It's along the lake, on the Wisconsin border."

"Is your family still there?"

"Yeah. My mom and brothers."

I see her looking at me. An inquisitive expression on her face.

"So why Madison. Why are you moving here?"

"Because …" I hesitate, probably too long, then say, "my best friend from high school is here. He's a student."

"That makes sense, so what is *your* plan up here?"

Not having thought things through, I scramble to come up with a response. A second later, I say, "Get a part time job and figure out if I want to go back to school." This answer was forced out of me, but it's true, I guess.

"Are you staying at your friends now?"

Another question I'm forced to answer. "Not really, I'm going to see my mom this weekend." Not knowing what else to say.

"Wonderful."

We walk along tree lined streets and soon start a slow climb up the aptly named Summit Street.

"I let things go after I lost Charles. I've got a list going—in case I ever decide to sell and follow friends to Arizona."

"How long have you lived in Madison?"

"Charles and I moved here right after we graduated. His job started three days later, here at U. W. So, it's been fifty-three years."

"Sounds like it would be hard to leave."

"To be honest, I was joking, I do not want to go to Arizona. I only want to mark off the projects on my list. I figure if I can help a young person out along the way, it will be a win-win."

We continue our climb. Lily is surprisingly fast. I must pick up my pace to keep up.

"That's my house ahead on the corner. The dark brick with green trim."

Wow, I think to myself … it's a charming looking home; two stories with a gabled roof shingled in wood. The whole neighborhood is filled with big homes in a variety of styles, no two alike. I don't know a lot about housing prices, but I'm sure this neighborhood isn't cheap; every yard is landscaped just so. "It's beautiful," I say. "How long have you lived here?"

"Thank you," she says. "It seems like I've been here forever. We closed on our fifth anniversary."

"That's some anniversary."

"Yes, it was, but we had to scrimp and save in those early years."

Together, we walk towards the side of the house and enter through the kitchen. She flips on music that starts playing on a sound system.

"You'll have to get used to that; it plays throughout the house. I love having soft music playing, as well as a candle burning. I try to engage all my senses."

"I like it," I say, inhaling lavender from a candle sitting on a warmer.

It feels strange to be in this kind woman's fancy home; I'm not used to being in a place so high-end. I'm not sure I'd fit in, but I'm grateful for her talking to me and showing me inside. I stand in place and gaze around.

A large island with two chairs sits in the kitchen. Stainless steel appliances throughout, the kitchen is housed in dark stained shaker cabinets and sage green tile. I can tell it's been renovated in the last few years. I like the look.

"Let me give you a tour of the place," she says as she slips on a pair of what she calls her "recovery shoes."

James Taylor plays while Lily shows me around the house. Our tour ends on the first floor, and Lily says, "Jack, this will be your room."

My mouth opens and a smile breaks out.

"What! Are you saying that you're offering me the job ... I mean the room. You don't need any kind of references or anything."

"No need." She pauses, then adds, "Honestly, Jack, I knew when I saw your smile."

"Wow!" I say, astonished. "Thank you."

My shock is quickly replaced by nerves.

Sitting on a banquette in the kitchen, eating a salad Lily threw together, she and I talk about the logistics of moving in. It is agreed that I will come back Monday morning with my things. There's no backing out now.

After we finish lunch, Lily walks me to the front door. A wall of books stands on one side of the tiled entryway.

"I like the books. That's quite a collection," I say.

"Do you like to read?" she asks, her brows raised.

"Yeah," I say, remembering a few assignments from my Intro to Philosophy course; those passages that made me think.

"I really like the plaid binding on these." I point to a couple dozen books, lined up next to one another.

Her face lights up. "My journals! I have been writing in those since I was twelve."

"Wow," I say, "That's incredible." All that she's experienced in life is here … in these volumes.

"They've been a part of me."

"Until Monday," she says as she reaches out for a hug.

Her embrace is tighter than I expect and lasts a few seconds.

"Thanks again," I say, as I walk out her front door.

"Enjoy your weekend at home."

"I will."

As I walk down her sidewalk, Lily calls out, "Can you stop by Colectivo and grab that flyer?"

"Sure thing!"

As I walk down Summit Street, I can't stop smiling. I'm nervous, but I'm also excited about moving into Lily's. I shake my head in amazement at what has transpired in the last couple of hours. I've gone from not knowing where I'd sleep tonight, to deciding to move to Madison. Surprisingly, I am most excited about getting to know Lily; she is kind, and from the little I've gleaned so far, has lived an interesting life.

A year from now, you will wish you had started today.

Quote written on the chalkboard at Colectivo Coffee

THREE / confess

June 19 –   Zion, Illinois

On my two-hour drive home, I think about what I will tell my mom about school. I know it will be a disappointment, and inside she'll be hurt, but outwardly, she'll be sympathetic (as always) and will be supportive. It's knowing that I'll hurt her that makes me sad. I turn up the music to drown out the negative thoughts.

"Hi, Mom," I say, as I walk through the screen door. I inhale something that smells delicious, her homemade tomato sauce.

"Jack!" my mom calls out as she stirs a pot on the stove in our small kitchen. My mom is as young as moms come, at least in my circle of friends; I was born when she was twenty. She smiles, her teeth straight from braces she started wearing at the same time as me. I walk over and hug her. She says, "Your brothers are in the basement."

"Hey Pat. Hey Jamie," I call out as I head down the stairs.

They are playing pool on the table mom bought us a few years back. The perfect purchase for three growing boys.

I ask how their summers are going, then I say, "Guess where I've been?"

After a couple of wrong guesses, I say, "Nope. California, Vegas, Colorado." All places mom has already taken us. "Brody and I took a road trip. It was awesome." I share more as I punch the speed bag while I wait to play the winner.

Patrick, four years younger, is home for the weekend, on a break from his job at a summer camp up north. Jamie, thirteen, has been alone and it's clear he misses having a brother around.

Later, I tell my mom that I got into a fight with Jimmy, and that's why I came home early. I tell her my plans about staying in Madison, "for the rest of the summer."

"How is grandma doing with her new hip?" I ask, pivoting the conversation. I don't want to get into anything about school yet. I end the conversation with, "We should talk later."

Over a dinner of lasagna and my favorite, warm crusty bread, I find I don't know much about my brothers. They share stories, and I find myself impressed. It's almost as if they were strangers. that's how little attention I have paid. I haven't been as close to them the past couple of years; we didn't run in the same circles but, honestly, it's because I have been too concerned with myself. I feel guilty for not staying connected to them … or my mom. Unsure now how to re-create those bonds.

As mom and I do the dishes, I spill the beans. I open up. I tell her about my struggles at school, copping to my priorities being out of whack. Being honest, a start to reconnecting. I tell her my plan about helping Lily in exchange for room and board.

"Why don't you move back home? You have room and board here, too, you know."

"I know mom. It's just … I know myself. If I move back home, I'll fall back into the same habits. It's too easy to be lazy, or at least, it is for me. I need a fresh start and to see what I can figure out."

After a few seconds, she says with a furrowed brow, "Okay. I understand."

She is probably worried I'll continue to drink too much, which I just told her I did at school, and worried I'll stay away from home for long stretches of time.

"I'll need to get a part-time job or something, but I'll make it work."

As we finish the dishes, mom says, "Before you leave Monday, I want to give you something."

"I can't wait."

I hang out at home for the rest of the weekend, playing video and board games with my brothers. Before I fall asleep Sunday night, I think what a great weekend it was; how nice it was to be with family. My last visit home wasn't as enjoyable. Then, I was sulking; depressed about the direction I was headed. My mind races with what can go wrong with my move. Maybe I can't complete the projects she has. Maybe I won't like living in a stranger's home and will be confined to that small room. Maybe her expectations are too high. Maybe I won't be able to find a part time job. Plus, I'm not currently speaking to the only other person I know in Madison.

My brothers and I are sitting at the kitchen table; they are up earlier than they'd like. My mom comes up from the basement carrying a well-used, but recently polished gray metal toolbox with Craftsmen spelled out in big red letters. With a tear in her eye, she hands me the familiar toolbox.

"There's a mix of old and new tools in here, and a new tool belt too."

"Thanks, Mom." I smile.

We walk out together. I throw my two duffel bags (my clothes, now clean), a backpack, and the toolbox into the back. I hug my brothers and tell them to, "enjoy the rest of the summer."

My mom hugs me and whispers into my ear, "I love you, Jack."

"I love you, too, Mom," I say, with a slight grin.

After I get in my car, mom hands me an envelope and says, "You can open it later."

I back up into the street, then give a final wave.

I open the envelope as soon as I turn off my street. Inside is a card with the quote, "No matter how hard the past, you can always begin again."

It's the perfect quote as I head towards a new life and a new opportunity. As I always do, I feel confident I will follow through *this* time, and make some improvements. Though I will be the first to admit, my success rate for reaching any goal I've set is not great. I like to plan and dream, but my follow-through has been lacking, to say the least.

I vow to maintain a positive mindset—and change my ways. At Northern, I was always focused on the distractions, the first to join anything that sounded fun, regardless of whether I had homework or class. Always saying to myself, I'll pull an all-nighter and get it done. I never did. The months passed and, like a snowball rolling downhill, my problem only got bigger. One day in my last semester, I realized it was past the point of no return. So, I solely focused on having a good time. I kept running, pushing the day of reckoning further and further away. It turns out my cross-country road trip was also *my* last hurrah. My dream was for a solo life on the road, me still running, but then Lily appeared.

FOUR / begin

June 22 –   Madison, Wisconsin

On the back roads to Madison, I devise a plan: read more, exercise more, and find a part-time job I enjoy. No more scrolling for hours on end, something I've always done. I envision a new life, focused and finding the confidence I lack.

I make it to Madison earlier than planned. I stop for a McDonald's coffee and drink it while I drive around Lily's neighborhood, University Heights, before pulling in her driveway five minutes early.

"Good morning, Jack! How was your trip?"

"Hi, Lily!" I say as I'm walking up her sidewalk. "It was good. A lot of time to think."

"Would you like some eggs? I was just about to scramble some."

"That would be great."

Over breakfast, Lily shares the highlights on her list. "Three rooms to paint, two of which need wallpaper removed. Build another raised garden bed. Paint the trim and shutters. Clear out the attic. That's at least a start."

My worry about not being able to do the work, returns.

After breakfast we walk out to the patio. Flowers are bordering her yard and two small, raised beds are near the back of her property.

"I'll need you to help me tend to the beds, and the yard as well."

"Of course." I say with a smile.

"There is no rush on any of this," she says as she hands me her list.

"Number one," I say, "build a raised garden bed."

"Gardening is something I've always enjoyed," she says. "And nowadays, that's where I spend my time, doing what I love." She adds, "I think I can get some more strawberries planted and harvested, yet this year."

"I can't wait to get started."

"You can go to Isthmus Hardware for anything you might need. Just tell them to put it on my account," she tells me. "I spoke to Harry. He's aware you're my new handyman."

Over the next few weeks, I spend each morning working on that day's project. Lily and I agreed it was a fair exchange for me to work four hours a day, five days a week.

I have come up with a system that works for me. First, I watch a few YouTube videos on my new project. I'll watch the best one a second time and take notes. I then take my shopping list to the hardware store and get what I need.

As an example; for the garden bed, I rewatched the same video more than a few times. I found the dimensions of the other two beds, to be sure mine matches exact. Two trips to bring back all the lumber, cedar of course. Measure twice, cut once—a lesson learned on day one. The frame takes three long days, but I'm an expert by the end. I fill it with soil, fertilizer, and then watch Lily plant. When she finishes watering her crop, she turns to me and says, "It's exactly what I'd hoped." A sense of pride washes over me, and I can't help but smile.

Depending on the project, I usually work an hour or two in the afternoon as well, though neither of us is keeping track.

I go for a long walk in the afternoons, normally about five miles. I've started reading, more than ever before; I'm sure seeing Lily reading every day has influenced me, plus I have her library from which to choose.

I first read Emerson at Lily's suggestion. Now I am reading *Walden;* these books make me think about life differently. She also showed me how she takes notes when she reads and has a file box, overflowing, with a collection of quotes and ideas she's saved. I, too, have started collecting ideas or anything that resonates with me. One of my favorites so far, Thoreau's quote, "Never look back, unless you are planning to go that way."

Most every night we have dinner together; our conversations are enjoyable. She asks questions about the books I'm reading, and we occasionally discuss past events in our lives. She can draw stuff out of me that I was unaware was there.

One night, over dinner, she asks, "Are you still journaling?" I can tell by the excitement in her voice, she hopes I am. I started to journal the first week I was here—writing about my day, and whatever comes to mind.

"Every night," I say with a smile, knowing she believes it to be worthwhile.

"Good." She nods her approval.

"I saw the wedding invitation on the counter. Who's getting married?"

"One of my students. She graduated towards the end of my career."

Lily taught at a local college; the campus is across from the Colectivo. I ask, "How long did you teach?"

"Over thirty years. I loved it."

"Were you always a professor?"

"No," she says, shaking her head. "I was a therapist when we first moved here. I had my master's in psychology. After a couple years of private practice, I did not get the satisfaction I was expecting. I wanted to help people, but I didn't feel it; except when I worked with adolescents."

"What was it about working with kids that you liked?"

"They are much more open," she says with a smile. "They're more receptive—and curious. But there weren't as many in therapy back then. That's why I wanted to teach. I liked the idea of mentoring young people, especially girls."

"So, when did you start teaching?"

"It took some time to make that change. At first, I didn't want to rock the boat with Charles. Things were going great for him at the University. Outwardly, I was happy." She hesitates, then says, "But inside, I wasn't. I was struggling to decide if I should pursue my dream of becoming a professor."

"What finally made you decide?"

"One day I was making breakfast—the same breakfast I had been making every day for years—over easy eggs, sausage, and toast. I remember looking down at *that* plate, and something inside me clicked. I said to myself, "This is silly. I can't keep reliving the same day." I hadn't said a word to Charles about wanting to teach but that afternoon I walked down to the graduate school admissions office and started the process which eventually led to my PhD."

"I love that," I say, feeling a bit humbled, as the idea of a job helping others has never crossed my mind. "It must feel great knowing the effect you've had on people."

"It does."

"I've only had a couple of teachers where I felt a real connection. It's a talent to impact someone like that."

I enjoy evenings like this. Before moving to Lily's, I'd spend my nights on my phone or streaming some meaningless show. Here, there's not a single television in the house. Now, if I'm not talking to Lily, I either read or write. Removing these distractions has helped me focus, giving me time to think. Lately, Lily and I sit in chairs in the living room near the stone fireplace reading or talking. Occasionally she offers me a glass of wine, but rarely more than one. I haven't been drunk once since I moved here. Now, I wake up feeling good.

A few days later Lily asks, "What are some of your favorite childhood memories?"

I think for a minute, then say, "Spending summers at a YMCA camp. I loved it, especially after becoming a counselor-in-training. I loved our family vacations too. They always involved camping; we spent many nights in the Northwoods. I remember drinking hot chocolate by the fire, chasing fireflies, or looking up to a starry sky. Those were some of the happiest times for me and my brothers," I say with a smile.

"Charles and I always wanted children, but they never came," Lily says. "I admit, it was difficult at first, but we grew to accept that us having kids was not meant to be."

"I'm sorry you weren't able to have any," I say with a frown.

"We both had fulfilling careers," she says, "and that helped."

I think of her in this house, alone since Charles' been gone. No kids—now, me here—to fill a void?

The days pass, and I progress on Lily's list. I finished painting the first bedroom and am now working on the second. I spend this afternoon working in the yard as Lily tends to her flowers. When I get back from my afternoon walk, I take a seat at the counter and watch Lily peel carrots.

"When we met, you said that you wanted to work on being a better person," she says, out of the blue.

"I remember," I say. Curious where this is headed.

"Have you identified what that better person looks like?"

"Not specifically," I say, still unsure, then add, "I think I was looking to be better in a general sense … just be nicer to the people in my life."

"You have improved in that area," she says. "I hear you talking to your mom and brothers."

"Yeah. It makes me feel good when I reach out."

"You also told me on that first day that you were upset with yourself for not working harder in school. Not focused enough."

"Yeah." I wonder if she views me as her student—or her patient.

"You have made progress there too," she says. "You are very conscientious when you work on a project."

I give her a smile. I'm glad she's noticed. I have been better at paying attention to the little things. I try to impress her every day. "I enjoy working with my hands," I say. "It's the first time I've really done this kind of thing."

I refill my water glass from the pitcher on the table. I refill Lily's glass too.

"Not only that," she says, "but as a person. I'm wondering with your journaling if you have gotten to know yourself better?"

"Sure, I think so. You talked about what I value, what's important to me. I have worked to identify those things."

"That's an important first step," she says. "Now, have you identified what areas of yourself you'd like to improve—what you're focusing on?"

"I'm not sure." I shrug.

"I guess what I mean, is, have you thought about the person you want to become?"

"Not really, but I guess I want to be successful. You know, not to have money worries."

"That's fine, but think about a few specific areas in your life, and how you want to approach them," she says. "I always focused on three areas: my relationships, my spirituality, and contributing to society."

"To be honest, I haven't spent much time thinking about any of those things, I say, shaking my head. "Well, except for the relationship with my mom."

"I understand," she says. "Everyone's different, but reflecting on what's important to you, will help you identify what path you should take in life. If that means finding a job that pays you well, that should be what you work towards. But that probably means going back to school. Are you ready for that?" She gives me a sideways smile.

Is she pushing me to go back to school?

"I hadn't given that much thought."

"Here's an idea, you should write a letter to your future self, say five years from now. Tell him where you hope he's at. Ask him what he would do different?" She pauses. "And, ask how he's treated others— since that was your first self-improvement goal."

An interesting assignment, me, five years from now. I have no idea who *that* guy will be, or where I'll even be living. Interesting to think about what *he'd* say to me, today.

The days start to pass quickly, not veering too far from my routine. I work in the morning, walk, and then back to my private space. My room is small, but there's a full-size bed, a dresser, a closet, and a small desk, that early on, Lily had me move in here. She told me her husband had written several books on it and would love for it to be used again. "It was always his favorite place to write," she said as she reached out to touch the desk. The only decoration in the room is a large black and white photograph of Yosemite.

This afternoon, I decide to write that letter to myself, five years in the future. It's harder than I thought, not having found a path I want to follow. I don't have a specific dream; I don't think that's normal. I start to compare. Jimmy, his plan to become a C.P.A. has been there since high school, freshman year; Brody's dream to go into advertising was there before we met; my plan heading to college was generic, business, never certain what that even meant.

So, the gist of the letter to my future self—I hope you have a good relationship with our family, good friends, time to travel, and be making a good living. I think to myself, I'd be happy with that.

When it is close to five, I sit at the kitchen counter, just as Lily is putting a casserole into the oven.

"It will be ready in thirty minutes," she says. "So, how was your day?"

"Great. I've got the last of the wallpaper off in the bedroom," I say. "Have you decided on a color?"

She hands me a paint swatch with one circled, Glacial Green.

"I'll pick up the paint tomorrow and get started."

During dinner Lily asks, "Would you like to watch a movie tonight?"

"Here?" I ask, surprised. "On what?"

"Yes," she says. "I'll show you after dinner. I have a few movies to choose from."

Once we finish the last of the dishes, she pulls open a drawer with maybe twenty movies. I've seen a few, but many are foreign films I don't know.

"I like *Groundhog Day*," I say.

"Me too," she says, smiling.

Lily pulls out a small projector and DVD player from a closet, then presses a button on the wall near the fireplace. A screen drops down from the ceiling.

"Popcorn?" she asks as she raises her brows and grins at me.

"Yay! Movie night," I say.

Lily and I laugh our way through the comedic gem.

I'd always liked the humor but never thought too deeply about it. Tonight, I watch it with a different set of eyes.

Afterwards, Lily asks me, as though I am one of her students, "What did you take away from the movie this time?"

"From a philosophical perspective," I say, "I think that doing your best every day will lead to a more meaningful life. Helping others. Making the most of the time you have."

"Those are some great lessons to learn," she says with a huge smile.

Most weekends I try to take at least one day trip someplace for a hike. Devil's Lake, an hour north, is one of my favorites as it's the only place in the area where I get any kind of climb. A trail runs along ridges which circle a stunningly blue lake. It is a five-mile hike with 1000 feet in elevation gain. Afterwards, I go for a swim in the lake. It makes for a perfect day. I've also been home twice to see my mom and brothers.

Reading and writing now fill most of my downtime. My writing is mostly stream of consciousness, not letting my pen leave the paper. I let everything in my mind spill on the page. Lily tells me, "A clear mind is fertile ground for new ideas." It's interesting what comes flowing out. Occasionally, I write some of my thoughts or ideas on an index card and add it to my collection.

The last one I wrote: "Walk outside in nature long enough and you'll never make your way back. Your ideas on life will change you from within."

I am in a much better state of mind. I think the reason I've been able to maintain good habits the last month is because I'm no longer in a place that triggers me to make unhealthy decisions. At school, I was always looking for a good time; and if there was a chance to meet girls, even better. At home, with my mom and brothers, lazy was my default. I had no energy to do much of anything.

Over dinner a couple of weeks later, Lily asks, "Have you called your friend in town?"

Lily knows about my fight with Jimmy, but in my telling the blame wasn't placed where it belonged.

"Not yet," I say. My guilt rising to the surface. "I will, but I am in a good place now. I don't want to mess it up."

"I'm not sure why talking to him would mess anything up."

I have not told Lily about the extent of my excesses in high school and college. But now I feel safe, thinking her judgement may be softened because she only knows the sober me.

"I never really told you about—let's say, my partying days."

"We all have had our youthful indiscretions," she says. "I was in college during the sixties, for Christ sakes." She flashes me a smile.

I smile at the thought of Lily in college, smoking a joint. "Good to know."

"So, tell me what you are afraid of."

"Well, before I moved here, I would drink a lot, usually before going out," I say. "I was always looking for the next fun thing. That's why I flunked out. That version of me was always chasing a buzz, be it booze or drugs. It was my way to escape. Heck, before I met you, I was ready to move into a van and keep running."

"It sounds like you're still running," she says with a caring grin.

"Maybe."

Is that true, am I still running?

"Anyways, in high school, Jimmy witnessed it all, but still supported me. Now, being around him reminds me of that time in my life."

"I would think you'd like him to see you, the new version."

"To be honest," I say, "I'm afraid I'd fall into my old habits. That's why I like it here, where there aren't any temptations."

"You can't stay locked away from the world, Jack."

Later, I'm on the couch reading when Lily walks in.

"I was thinking about when we met," she says.

"Yes," I say, "I *was* hungover."

"I could tell, but that's not where I'm going. What I want to tell you is that we all need help from time to time. I know it's not easy. Do you know how long it took me to finally hang that flyer?"

I shake my head.

"After Charles died, I couldn't do much of anything. I sat in the house," she says, "turning away friends who only had the best of intentions. I let things go around here. It has *never* been easy for me to ask for help. I had the idea to find a handyman for over a year, but I couldn't bring myself to ask."

"I didn't realize."

"And speaking of help, I am going to give you some cash for all the extra stuff you've been doing."

I've done some driving for her. Taking her to a few doctors' appointments, those where she can't drive afterwards, and running a few errands, including a dozen trips to Goodwill.

"No need," I say. "Lily, you've been more than generous."

"Jack, let me tell you something," she says in a mock, scolding tone. "You need to learn to accept kindness, if not for yourself, for the person making the offer. It's a lesson I learned too late in life."

"I get it."

"It makes the giver feel happy, giving a gift you know someone will love."

I already feel like a charity case but offering me money for simply caring is a bit offensive, though I appreciate her offer.

"I hear you. But for the record, I'm actually pretty thrifty and still have money saved."

The words trigger a memory that flashes in my mind. A friend in college responds to me calling myself "thrifty" with, "You're not thrifty. You're cheap. There's a difference." He continues, "You rarely contribute your fair share, and you did it again last night at dinner." His comment stung but was on point. I didn't have a lot of cash, having spent too much earlier on my drinks. Instead of coming clean, I toss less than I should have onto the table when the bill came. That pain resurfaces now.

I decide to share the story with Lily.

She responds, "Being honest with yourself is not always easy. It's a lesson that hopefully people will learn early, though some never do."

A bit later Lily says, "I'm planning a little party in a few weeks, and I would like you to be one of my guests?"

"I'd be honored."

"I finally feel good about having people over again," she says. "I had let all those little things around the house get to me. Now, thanks to you, my mind is clear."

"I'm glad I could help."

"Bringing people together," she says smiling, "it's something I've always loved doing."

"Dinner," she tells me, "will be you, me and my friends, Mary, Ben, Steven, and Emily. I will need your help with a few things if you don't mind." She lists what she'll need. I haven't seen Lily this excited about anything.

"I'll be happy to help."

"Ben is *now* the head of the Philosophy Department. He wants to look through some of Charles's papers. I'm hoping you can look for them in the attic. Then you two can work on getting him what he wants."

"Sure," I say. "So, were Charles and Ben friends."

"Yes, they worked together for a long time. We also hung out as couples. Ben's wife passed away the year after Charles."

"Are you and Ben … *close*?" I ask suggestively.

"Not like that," she says, shaking her head. "Ben is a good man, but I could not have been married to him. He is too particular about things." In a hushed tone, she adds, "And a little too ostentatious for my taste."

There has been no talk of how long our work exchange will last, though Lily once said, "You're welcome to stay as long as it takes to find your direction in life." It's clear to both of us that I haven't found it yet. For now, I value each day I'm here.

> *There is a time in every man's education when he arrives at the conviction that envy is ignorance; that imitation is suicide; that he must take himself for better, for worse ... The power which resides in him is new in nature, and none but he knows what that is which he can do, nor does he know until he has tried.*
>
> Ralph Waldo Emerson, *Self-Reliance*

FIVE / dinner

The fireplace is glowing. Soft jazz is playing. An orange sky is visible out Lily's front window. There are five of us gathered in the living room talking. I'm still on my first glass of wine. I'll be sure to watch my drinking tonight.

Lily chimes her glass and says, "Let's head into the dining room."

After everyone else is seated, Lily, who remains standing, says, "I'm having this dinner catered by Sara." She raises her arm toward a young woman standing in the doorway to the kitchen. "She did all the cooking and chose our wine for tonight. Now, I'd like everyone to tell Sara goodnight. She said she'd be happy to stay and serve, but I told her we could manage."

As we're saying our goodnights, Lily says, "I was at a dinner last month, which Sara had catered. It was *amazing*. I wanted a reason to enjoy another of Sara's meals, so here we are."

"I hope you enjoy the food!" Sara says with a wave.

Next to me is Mary, Lily's best friend. Steven is sitting across the table. He and his wife, Emily, are longtime friends of Lily. He is now Lily's financial adviser, after having taken over his dad's firm. Steven came alone tonight.

Lily and I serve the plated first course. As we are sitting down, Ben stands and says, "Will everyone please raise your glass to Lily for bringing us together this evening."

"To Lily," we say in unison.

Lily blushes and nods.

Everyone clinks one another's glasses. As we do, I stare at my glass.

"Jack," Lily whispers. "Be sure to look the other in the eye." Another "pointer" as Lily and I have begun calling these tips on proper etiquette.

Ben looks at Steven and says, "I'm sorry Emily couldn't make it."

"Me too. She had another last-minute meeting in Palo Alto and flew out this morning."

Ben has remained standing. As he and Lily make eye contact, he says, "I've known you for almost forty years. I can honestly say I have never met a stronger woman than you. I'm so glad you've made it through the last two years with your smile still intact."

When Ben is seated, Mary stands up and says, "Well, I've known Lily for over thirty-four years, and she's my best friend. I love you, Lily." Mary's eyes well with tears.

Steven says, remaining seated, "Well Lily, what, we've known each other for maybe twenty-five years, and close friends for the last fifteen."

"It's been a long time," she says. Then looks at me and adds, "Steven once said I was his only client who befriended his wife." Lily turns toward Steven and says, "Maybe you and Emily can stop by next week. I'd love to see her."

Since everyone else has said something, I feel I should too. I am not comfortable speaking in front of others, even this small of a group. After a few moments of silence, I say, "My turn, I guess. Well, I met Lily a whopping seventy-five days ago. Time has flown by; I can't believe it's been that long."

I know I spoke way too fast and feel a bit self-conscious.

Then I turn to Lily and say, "Thank you for inviting me tonight."

Mary puts her hand on my arm and says, "Even though we just met, I feel like I know you." She and Lily talk every day, so I'm sure she's heard stories.

As we eat our first course, Lily says, "Mary, tell Jack where the Hoofers are going next week."

"We're hiking part of the Ice Age Trail. Have you done any hiking along that route?"

"No. I normally head to Devil's Lake. And what exactly are the Hoofers?"

She laughs. "You've got to expand your horizons, Jack. There are lots of nice trails around here," she says. "And, Hoofers is an outdoors group attached to the University, but locals can join too. I've been a member for over twenty years. I belong to their skiing club, but I go on hiking and other fun outings."

"Sounds cool."

"I hear you like to take walks around town," Mary says, looking at me.

"I do. I usually walk through campus to the Capitol building. But sometimes I go to the Arboretum."

"Well, I have on offer for you."

"What's that?"

"Take my dog, Vita, along with you," she says with a pretty-please smile. "I'll pay you the going rate for dog walkers. Mine is moving."

Wow, I think—I've been dragging my feet on getting a part-time job, not wanting to take time away from anything I'm doing right now. But this could be great. I say, "I think I could do that."

"Fantastic! We can discuss the logistics after dinner."

Lily and I leave the table and return with the main course.

"Crab cakes, my favorite," Steven exclaims, rubbing his hands together.

"I know," Lily says matter-of-factly. "When Sara served those as an appetizer, I immediately thought of you."

"Thank you," he says with a huge smile.

After a few bites of crab, Steven says, "My oldest daughter, Lauren, is your age. She goes to U-dub. She took last year off, but is now back, as a sophomore."

"What did she do on her year off?"

"Traveled. She took a couple of long trips overseas."

"Wow, that's great," I say. "I'd like to do that someday."

"I think it was good for her."

Steven raises his voice, to get everyone's attention, and says, "Lauren told Emily and I she no longer wants to go into finance. She said she's in the process of changing majors."

"That's a good thing," Lily says. "She shouldn't follow in your footsteps."

"What did she change her major to?" I ask.

"Actually, I'm not sure. She told my wife last night."

Lily looks at me and says, "I don't think Steven's happy I suggested to Lauren that she take a gap year."

"I just said it was good for her," he says as he turns up his hands and chuckles.

I share with Steven how I ended up in Madison. He listens intently and then he shares stories of his "university" years.

"I studied more than most, but still had lots of fun times. But I felt pressure to get good grades and an advanced degree. Then, after graduation, lots of long hours as I moved up the ladder," he says with a frown. "Lily mentioned Lauren following in my footsteps—well that's exactly what I did with my father, and there were times I've regretted it."

He tells me while he's finally managed to reduce his workload, his wife hasn't. I can sense he's not exactly thrilled with the situation.

Later, Ben asks from across the table, "Will you pass me the wine, Jack?"

I lean forward and stretch the bottle of wine to Ben.

He says, "Lily tells me she's your literary guide."

"Well, she's been recommending books, so I guess you can call her that."

"What have you read so far?"

"Let's see—Emerson, Thoreau, *The Alchemist*, *The Razor's Edge*, *Don Quixote*, a couple of Tolstoy's shorter ones, *The Death of Ivan Ilyich*, and few short stories," I respond. "I'm working my way through *Meditations* now."

"That's a good one," Ben says. "But Lily, why no Dostoyevsky—*Brothers Karamazov*? It's the greatest novel ever written. At least in my opinion."

"He'll get to it, I assure you," Lily says, looking at me.

Steven adds, "I have been meaning to re-read that book. It's been about ten years. I look forward to discussing it at a future gathering."

"Jack, have you attended any good lectures yet?" Ben asks.

"I don't go to school here," I respond, feeling something resembling shame.

"I realize that, but that doesn't mean you should stop learning. There are great lectures on campus all the time."

"That's good to know," I say. "Not counting classes in a lecture hall, I've never been to a quote lecture."

"A friend in the Architecture department recommended I attend one next week. It will be given by an expert on New Urbanism. If you'd like, we could go together."

After a second of silence, "Sure, I'd like that." I was surprised by the invitation, and even more so by my response. My first thought was—I don't even know him—but then I recalled the quote, "Life begins outside your comfort zone."

"Besides lectures, you're free to sit in on any philosophy class you think you might enjoy. If anyone asks, tell them, "Professor Virtanen suggested it.""

"Thanks! I'll do that," I say. Ben is nice, but his demeanor shows he's used to being in charge.

Over dessert, Ben says to Lily, "It's clear you're trying to remake yourself with young Jack here."

"Far from it," Lily scolds. "Jack is becoming his own man."

"No?" Ben says questioningly. "Okay then, maybe you're trying to turn him into, what in *your* head is, the ideal man."

"There may be a kernel of truth in that statement," she admits.

I'm not surprised by this conversation. It's been obvious since my first week here that Lily is guiding me, trying to nudge me in certain directions, but I don't take offense. I appreciate what she is doing for me.

I volunteer, "I'm not sure about the ideal man part, but I have made some improvements in my life—my habits have improved since I moved in."

Steven says, "We are what our habits create."

"Yeah, it's interesting to me how someone becomes the person they end up being in the end. I've thought about that a lot the last couple of months. I think spending time on productive activities, like reading and exercise, has me thinking about the future more positively than I did before."

"You reap what you sow," Mary offers. "Keep spending your time wisely, Jack. It will pay off in the end."

"Good to know."

After more conversation centered on some of their mutual acquaintances, Lily says, "It's getting late," and stands from her place at the head of the table. "I want to thank you all for coming tonight."

Conversations continue as everyone says their goodbyes.

After Lily closes the front door, she says, "I'm pooped."

"I hope you enjoyed meeting everyone," she says as she stacks the dessert plates.

"I did. It was great. Everyone was very kind," I say, gathering the coffee cups.

"You made a great impression."

"Thanks, I hope so," I say, though I'm not so sure.

"We'll do the dishes tomorrow. I need to get to bed."

As Lily walks up the stairs, she turns and says, "Good night, Jack."

"Good night."

As I lay in bed, I think that this has been one of the most "stimulating" evenings of conversation I've ever had. I now understand why it's called that; it stimulates the brain to think.

I was nervous a few hours ago about meeting Lily's friends. I knew they were all successful, and I hadn't lasted even two years at school.

Drinking had been my crutch for social situations like tonight, but I think I did okay. I appreciate Lily introducing me to her friends. I'm sure they were all aware of our arrangement before, and she wanted *them* to meet *me*.

Before I doze off, I smile, excited that I now have a way to earn some money and about meeting my new walking partner tomorrow.

> *When we strive to become better than we are, everything around us becomes better too.*
>
> Paulo Coelho, *The Alchemist*

SIX / fall

October 19 –   Madison, Wisconsin

"I was shocked when I saw you walking towards me—with two dogs nonetheless," Jimmy says.

"Yeah, I can see that," I say with a big smile.

We are on the terrace of the Union at one of its colorful tables, sitting on unique chairs, the backs and seats carved with a sunburst; everything a vibrant orange, yellow, or green. We look out on Lake Mendota; a handful of small sailboats are out on the water. There is not a cloud in sight. We ran into each other on campus two minutes ago and headed straight here.

"I can't believe you didn't tell me you were living here," he says with a look of confusion.

"Yeah, I know," I say with a wince. "It's just that I have been doing good lately, staying in my little bubble." Jimmy and I have not spoken or even so much as texted since *that* night.

"That's good to hear, Jack. I'm happy for you," he says with a smile. "And what exactly do you mean by 'your bubble'?"

"Well, I've been spending time with some older folks, and working on myself. I haven't been going out."

"I've been wondering," he says. "So, what's up with the dogs?"

"I am now a part-time dog walker. It's like I get paid to listen to audiobooks and go for a walk," I say with a shrug. "A few months ago, I moved here and started walking Vita," pointing her out. "And Finn here for the past month or so."

"What were you listening to?" I had my new Air Pods in earlier.

"This will surprise you," I say. "A book by Friedrich Nietzsche."

"Really? Why?"

"I've done a lot of reading, and it's led me to a lot of different stuff."

"So, where are you staying?"

"Funny story. Do you remember that day I left your place?"

"Yeah, of course."

I give him a rundown on what's happened since.

"Damn, you've got a pretty good setup. Saving money and everything."

"Trust me, I know. I'm grateful for Lily."

"How much longer will she need a handyman?"

"Well, I've completed most everything on her list, but she keeps finding new projects," I say. "I still do her yard work and run errands for her. She's even farmed me out to a couple of her friends."

"I'm happy for you, Jack," he says, patting my shoulder.

"Thanks, I appreciate it."

Jimmy tells me what's been going on with him, mostly academics, as that's his focus in life right now. He tells me his mom, who has M.S., is starting to struggle more.

I've thought a lot about the people in my life lately. What I've come to understand about Jimmy is, he simply wants to make his "dying" mom proud. That's what drives him.

"I have been drinking less," I volunteer. I still care what he thinks.

"That's good," he says. "I know you like having a good time, but it's nice to see you happy, sober."

"It hasn't been hard," I confess. "I've confined myself to Lily's, so I don't have the temptation. I realized the only reason I drank so much before was to be more social, especially with girls. I never really drank alone, just in anticipation of going out. Here, I don't go out."

"You can't stop going out forever," he says with a shrug.

"You're right," I say with a little laugh, knowing he's always looked out for me.

Over the last months, I've thought about my relationships, especially my relationship with Jimmy. Guilt for not being the friend I should have been, was always just beneath the surface. I have been thinking about reaching out to him for weeks, but it got harder as the days passed. There are things I wanted to say. This is my opportunity.

In a serious tone I say, "I need to apologize to you. I've always been the taker," flashing air quotes, "in our friendship. You were the one that always reached out, making sure we stayed in touch. I was lazy about it. I've been thinking a lot lately and I was always a bit jealous of you, the achiever. You've always been a bit smarter, better with the girls, and the rest of the crowd. And, of course, the hardest worker I know. It made me feel bad to be around you sometimes. I took out my insecurities on you. I just want to tell you that. And I'm sorry."

He nods his head and smiles. "I appreciate you telling me. I know things haven't been easy for you." He looks me in the eye and pats my forearm. "You've always been my best friend. I love you, man."

"I love you, too," I say, my eyes welling with tears.

"Well, I have to get to class," he says. "We should get together soon."

"I'd like that. I *WILL* text you."

"Sounds good. I'll see you," he says with a wave.

A few days later, I get a text from a friend at Northern, Dylan, who I haven't heard from since early Spring semester. *I hear you're up in Madison. Me and Luke are gonna be there Thursday. You wanna hang?"*

I liked going out with them. It was always a good time; we'd usually be out until dawn. I get a rush of adrenaline thinking about those nights. I text back, *Sure, I'm down.*

I must be careful, knowing myself, but I do want to go out with the *cool* guys. These two are at college just to have fun—but who am I to judge. They're both big on Instagram and have only seemed to care about gaining more followers.

My phone pings. *Perfect. Can we crash?*

Of course, I think to myself, I should have known. I text back, *I'll let you know.*

Now what?

I decide one night will be okay. I am excited about a night out. Over dinner, I say to Lily, "I have a couple friends, brothers, coming to town Thursday. I was wondering if they could sleep in spare room?"

"Of course, Jack. But remember, I have an appointment Friday morning?"

"Don't worry, I'll get you there by 9:00." I smile. "I promise."

The three of us stumble back to Lily's at 3:00 AM.

A knock on my door.

A minute later, another knock.

The door opens. "Jack, I'm leaving now. I called an Uber."

I look up at Lily in the doorway. "I'm sorry."

Fuck!

I get out of bed and find Dylan and Luke passed out in the living room. One on the floor, the other on the couch. Two empty wine bottles on a side table.

"Hey! Get up," I say loudly. I shake them until they're awake.

"You guys have got to go."

"What's the problem?" Luke says.

"You drank her wine—and look at this place." I say, glancing around.

"It's no big deal," Dylan says.

"Are you *fucking* kidding me?" I scream. "This is my life. She lets me stay in her home. I don't have the luck to live like you too. Your futures are set." They have a family business waiting for them.

"Please leave." They get up to go.

I walk over and open the front door.

Luke looks at me and says, "Later, Jack."

"I don't think so. Lose my number."

I'm pissed at them.

I'm more pissed at myself.

I clean up the mess and shower. I think about what to say to Lily.

Waiting ... I get more nauseous by the minute.

She walks in the kitchen door.

I'm sitting at the counter.

As soon as we make eye contact I say, "I'm sorry."

"You should be," she says with downturned lips. "Do you know the vase you broke was a gift from Charles on our twentieth anniversary?"

"I didn't," I say, shaking my head. "I feel like shit. There's no excuse."

"I need to take some time."

"I get it."

She heads to her room.

I head to mine.

I sit in my room, nervous, wanting to give her space.

I spend the afternoon worrying I may have cost myself a great thing. I think about my drinking, and not knowing when to stop. Why do I do it? I don't have an answer.

Hours later, Lily knocks on my door.

"Come in."

"Dinner in an hour?"

"Yes, thanks." I have a feeling a dread.

I take a seat at the island. "I've thought about a lot this afternoon. It was an eye opener, falling into old habits. I knew deep down I would get carried away. I should have said something to you."

She nods.

"If I did, maybe you could have stopped me."

"No, Jack. These are lessons that need to be learned."

"No excuse," I say. "I just couldn't say no. I knew they were users; always have been."

"I know the type." Lily says with a nod. "But we all make decisions, and we have to live with them."

"I understand," I say, scared about what she might say next. I try to explain, "I'd always had fun with them, and I kind of missed that. I don't think I realized it until they called." The truth.

"Drinking often makes us do thoughtless things."

Ouch! She nailed it, that's exactly what it was. Selfish, yet again.

"I know that," I say. "I was proud when I moved here, and I was able to stop."

"I admit, last night took me by surprise," she says.

I nod my head and purse my lips. Still afraid of what she might say next.

"I know it's tough. We all have our things, things we crave."

"I guess. But I don't crave booze. I think it's just having a good time."

"You may need to self-medicate to have your fun."

"I don't think so," I say. "I have fun with my brothers, and I had fun in college, playing with my team and spending time with friends, all without a buzz."

"It may be your confidence is still lacking."

I look at her and smirk, "No doubt."

"I admit, it has given me pause. But you are aware, and that's a good thing."

It seems she is leaning towards forgiveness.

"I know I broke a promise. But I hope I didn't break your trust."

"No, Jack, that you still have."

A few days later, as I walk into the kitchen for breakfast, Lily says, "Did you finish your morning routine?"

"I did!" I have done pushups, pull-ups, and some yoga moves. "I hit fifty-five push-ups this morning."

"Remember Jack. No shortcuts."

"Yep. Just a little better today," I say proudly.

Our relationship seems back on solid ground.

"By the way, I won't be home for dinner tomorrow," she says.

"Me neither, I am going to my brother's game Where are you headed?"

"Ben and I are having dinner," she says coyly.

"Oo la la," I say, "Is this a date?"

"I hope so," she says with a grin. "He may get lucky." She gives me a little smirk.

My eyes widen and a smile washes over my face. I'm speechless.

"I haven't been on a *date* since Charles and I started out."

"So, how did you and Charles meet?" I say to change the subject.

"He was in a band in high school. We met at a party he and his friends were playing. He was the lead singer and played the guitar. It was love at first sight," she says with a grin. "Just looking at him, I went weak in the knees."

"How long before you started dating?"

"We were together since that first night. I haven't kissed another since."

"I saw a guitar case in the attic while bringing down the last of Charles' boxes. I meant to ask if I could bring it down. I thought I might give it a try."

"I was hoping that was there," she says. "That was his guitar, and of course you can have it. Put it to good use."

"Is it the one from *that* night?"

"The same one," she smiles.

"Wow," I say. "I love that story."

"Me too."

"I don't want to bother you with my bad playing." A serious concern.

"It's no bother. I would love to listen to you play. It will be fascinating to hear your progression."

Lily slides two eggs onto a plate and hands it to me. "I haven't mentioned to you, but I'm going to Europe for a few weeks in the Spring. I'm visiting some longtime friends."

"That sounds like a lot of fun. I hope to travel overseas someday," I say. "Speaking of Europe, I found a book on your shelves, *Walking Europe, Top to Bottom*, or something like that. I was wondering why you had it?"

"Oh, I've kept that for years. I saw it when I was much younger, and I thought maybe Charles and I could walk it together once he retired," she says. "It had been hard to part with that dream."

"I looked through it. It's mostly logistics; it wasn't a story like I'd hoped. But still cool."

After breakfast, Lily says, "Be sure to say hello to Vita and Finn for me. I'm headed to the beauty shop."

"Have a great day, Lily."

I wake from a dream, one that I want to return to. My alarm clock shows 2:17. I lay back onto my pillow and fight to keep the memory of the dream alive. I am traveling someplace I've never been, and I wake to find my shoes gone, my pack gone. I feel my pockets, my wallet and phone are here. In the dream, I'm confident everything will be okay. I walk out of an unfamiliar building into an early morning light. I spot an arrow, yellow, and start walking, barefoot, in the direction it's pointing. This is when I woke up.

After a few minutes of unsuccessfully trying to fall back asleep, my mind racing, I decide to write down my dream. I get out of bed, pull the brass chain on the desk lamp, and write what I remember of it. I try to make sense of what my subconscious is telling me.

Like in the dream, I'm on a quest to find something unknown, but in my life, there is no arrow pointing out my direction. I must find my path forward and leave behind stuff I don't need. My life, my story—I want to document my journey to becoming the person I want to be.

Around 10:00 the next morning, I walk up State Street, the Capitol building in view, to meet Jimmy for coffee. I texted him when I woke up, asking if he wanted to meet. I miss hanging out with him; he was my only close friend in high school, but I've only seen him a handful of times since the summer after graduation.

My breath is visible as I walk through recently fallen leaves blowing at my feet. I feel excited by the simple thought that this life is mine to create.

> *No one can build you the bridge on which you, and only you, must cross the river of life. There may be countless trails and bridges and demigods who would gladly carry you across; but only at the price of pawning and forgoing yourself. There is one path in the world that none can walk but you. Where does it lead? Don't ask, walk!*
>
> Friedrich Nietzsche, *Schopenhauer as Educator*

SEVEN / winter

December 17 –   Rib Mountain, Wisconsin

Snow is falling, big flakes floating with the breeze. I look out onto the valley below, the soft golden hour light masked by a bank of lights pointed down on the slope.

"Watch oooout!" I screech, as I almost run into a skier slaloming down the hill. This is my first-time skiing, and I am not good at slowing down yet.

Let me update you on what's been going on the last couple of months. First off, I've been practicing the guitar for hours each day. It's my newest passion. It's amazing what you can learn on YouTube.

I still walk my two friends almost every day.

My writing is coming along. I have written a few essays on various topics. The last one was about how having a creative release—be it music, writing, art, sketching, photography, etcetera—opens you up, so the artist within can break out.

After a life without any artistic endeavor, I now have two.

Lily reads my writing, then gives me her opinion and advice. She asked if she could share my writing with Mary.

I continue to make my way down a hill that feels bigger than it looks from a distance. Rib Mountain is the tallest in the state. I've learned to lean and put more weight on my outside ski to make a turn. I've found downhill skiing to be one of the most exhilarating things I've experienced.

I'm here, thanks to Mary who invited me along. She told me these trips are fun, and I am having a blast. This is the first time I've really ventured outside my little bubble.

The biggest news, I guess, is I've decided to take a long walk in Europe. I will follow the route in the book I found on Lily's bookcase. I'm enjoying my time at Lily's, and I like my routine, but I have been craving an adventure. Walking in a foreign land seems like just the thing. I fly out in June; I just sent off my passport application.

I use the "snowplow" stop as I near the bottom of the hill. My first, and only, attempt at the much cooler "skid" stop ended with me on the ground with a face full of snow. So, I went back to the easiest to master. This was my last run of the day, and my first under the lights. Soon our bus will take us back home. Mary, my instructor, says I picked this up quick. I'm not so sure, but at least now I can stop without running into things. I'm grateful that Mary introduced me to this sport. It's one she's enjoyed her whole life.

The days and weeks pass, following much the same routine.

One morning in the kitchen, Lily notices me gently rubbing my fingers together and says, "Is that from the guitar?"

"Yes," I say with downturned lips.

"Charles had rough fingers all his life. I remember him telling someone to put rubbing alcohol on their fingers to speed up building the calluses, so it's not as painful."

"Thanks, I'll try that," I say. "So, did Charles play the guitar all his life."

"Less and less," she says. "But he always liked to sing. I think that was always his biggest regret, not pursuing his music."

"How about you?" I ask. "What were your dreams when you were my age?"

"Horses!" She says instantly. "I loved to ride."

"I have noticed a couple pictures of horses around, but I didn't know they were a big part of your life."

"When I was young, my father read me the book *Black Beauty*. After that, I fell in love with them. For years, horses were all I cared about," she says wistfully. "As I got older, I didn't dream of a knight in shining armor, I envisioned a life with my horses."

"Did you have them here in Madison?" I ask.

"No, they stayed in PA after we married," she says. "I lost that part of myself." She stays quiet for a few seconds, then adds, "I had to take a backseat to Charles many times, and his dreams became my dreams. But once I started teaching, I started to feel more like me."

"I didn't realize." I walk toward the fridge, under the pretext of getting some orange juice, on the way, I stop and put my arm around Lily and give her a squeeze.

She smiles at me and says, "That was not uncommon in my day. Honestly, I can't think of anything I would change. I loved him with all my heart."

"When was the last time you went riding?"

"Oh my … it's been years."

"Why don't we go?" I say with a smile. "I'll find a place in the Spring."

"Let me think about it," she says with a nod. "My body is not what it was." She adds, "So, Jack, what are *your* dreams for the future?"

I take a few long seconds to think, then say, "To keep working on being that 'better person'." I think to myself, I don't know where that answer came from. I am paying attention to becoming more well-rounded, but I didn't realize that was my dream. A second later I add, "I guess to travel, too."

"I liked your first response." Then she asks, "Are you nervous about your trip?"

"A little, but I am excited for the adventure. I want to see if I can do it."

"It will be life changing."

Tomorrow I'm headed home for Christmas. Lily is flying to Stowe, Vermont to celebrate the holidays with Charles' sister.

On my first night back home, I'm chopping vegetables on our butcher block counter, while my mom cuts up the chicken for tonight's stir fry dinner. The wok is heating up on the stove.

"You seem to be in a good place. I was worried about you."

"Me too," I say. "But I'm doing great now." It feels good to say that and mean it. "And I've learned a lot."

"Stuff your dad should have taught you."

"I know mom," I say, touching her forearm. Acknowledging her wish that she could have done more to teach what other boys are taught. My mom's dad, with whom she was close, was a carpenter and ever so handy. I remember him is his workshop when I was maybe ten. A year later, he was gone. I remember how hard that was on my mom.

"So how is Jimmy?" she asks.

"He's good," I say. "His priority is the same as in high school." Then add, "Have you seen his mom, lately?"

"Last week I went over and cut her hair. She's taken a turn for the worse."

"That's sad," I say. "Jimmy mentioned that."

Over my two-week break I go sledding with my brothers, tackle a few of mom's projects, and just hang out. It's not until after Christmas that mom asks if I plan on going back to school.

"I still don't know," I say. "I'm going to take my walk and then figure things out."

"Jack, do what makes you happy, even if it means not going back to school."

I know she would prefer that I graduate. Neither she nor my dad went to college; they both went into the hair business.

On New Year's Eve, in our hometown, Jimmy and I head to a party at one of his high school friend's houses. We talk about my upcoming trip on the way, and he says, "I'm jealous."

Then he says, "I've been jealous of you most of my life. Your family was always fun—while mine, well it just wasn't." His home life was very somber. His mom has been confined to a hospital bed in the living room since our sophomore year. Her life limited to romance novels and listening to Jimmy play the piano; he was his teacher's star pupil.

We share recollections of the past and laugh most of the way over to the party. I love the level of our relationship now. It's more honest, being truer with our feelings. Plus, I feel better for carrying more of the weight in our friendship.

After two beers, my self-appointed limit, I walk across the living room and stumble into a wine bottle. It spills onto a rug. I quickly pick it up and place it back on the table. I look around to see if anyone saw. I don't think they did.

For a split second I think of walking away, but decide to, "speak the truth." I find the host and explain what happened. I tell him I will take care of the costs to have it cleaned or replaced.

He responds, "No worries—really." He looks me in the eyes and says, "Thanks for telling me."

I have a warm feeling in my chest. Proud I handled the situation the way I did, knowing in the past I would have run. Like a flip of a switch, somewhere along the way, I've changed.

***

In the dead of winter, I find myself inside the cocoon of Lily's house for days at a time. On these frigid winter days, the dogs do their business in their own backyards. My routine keeps me in good spirits. Every item on Lily's list has now been marked complete.

Over breakfast, I say, "The attic and garage are both empty. There's nothing left to add to your list."

She assures me, "There is no need to start paying rent." Despite our now, one-sided exchange.

I've thought about when I should leave, on more than a few occasions. The thing is, I've grown comfortable with our routine, probably too comfortable. I love Madison, a real university town, and I feel connected to the outdoors here, more than anywhere else I've lived. I don't want to leave this city, nor do I want to leave Lily's. I feel like I should come up with a plan, but decide to wait until I return from my trip.

"You're headed to Arizona, aren't you?" I ask.

"No, Jack, I am not, I promise," She responds laughing. "I'm sure I'll be in this house forever."

***

It is a Saturday in early April, outside Lily's window the trees are covered in green. Lily and I walk into the dining room with Sara, the incredible chef. Lily says to those gathered, "Sara just asked if the last guest had cancelled. I assured her that wasn't the case, and not to worry."

Then she adds, "You see, Sara will be our final guest. When Jack told me about Brody coming, I knew exactly what I would do." Lily had mention to me before, she likes an even number of guests.

Sara's expression shows her surprise.

Brody texted me last week and said he would be in the area. Lily kindly added him to her guest list.

Once the first course is out, Ben says, "Thank you for hosting us tonight, Lily. I'm glad to see everyone here, especially Emily, Lauren, and Alyssa (Lauren's younger sister). It's been a while. And it's been a pleasure meeting Brody."

Over dinner, Brody shares some semi-embarrassing stories of our college days, but overall, he is generous to my reputation. Brody is a great storyteller.

Later, I overhear him say to Steven, "Jack and I planned on writing a screenplay based on the road trip we took out west last summer."

"What made your trip story worthy?" he asks.

"Well, our weekend in Las Vegas was a highlight, however I can't share that story at the table. But we made some friends in the canyons of Utah, swam in the ocean, hiked the Tetons, and climbed Half Dome in Yosemite. It was unreal."

I sit next to Lauren, who tells me she plays volleyball. "Now just in a rec league, but I played in high school."

"I played in college too, like you," I say. "It was my favorite thing to do."

She tells me of her travels last year, and I share my upcoming plans.

Later, Steven says, "After our last dinner, I re-read Brothers Karamazov. Who here has read it?"

Five at the table have, and we attempt to convince those that haven't, they should.

"It's my new favorite book," I say. "Reading it gives you a fuller understanding of people; how we behave, think, and what drives us."

A few minutes later, Ben says, while looking at Lauren, "The books you read matter."

"Mom made me read *Little Women* in high school. I liked it. *Pride and Prejudice,* too," she says, "and I loved *The Alchemist*. I read it at a hostel in Greece."

I say, "I *love* Russian literature. I really liked *Crime and Punishment*; the way you're inside Raskolnikov's head is fascinating."

"You might like Herman Hesse," Ben offers. "I enjoyed, *Narcissus and Goldman*."

Sara and I gather the dinner plates and bring them into the kitchen.

"I'm sorry we haven't had a chance to talk," I say. "But dinner was amazing. Have you been cooking for a long time?"

"Thanks," she says. "Yes, I started taking classes in high school. They offered culinary classes for high school students at the Tech, so I took the bus there in the afternoons. I think I took every class they offered." She opens the dishwasher, and we start loading the dishes.

"What made you fall in love with food?"

"Cooking with my grandma," she says smiling.

"She's Italian, so we would make every kind of homemade pasta and sauce."

"That's awesome," I say. "Is this your full-time job?"

"It is now," she says with a smirk. "It's taken a few years to get here. It's almost all been through word of mouth. There were some rough times, but I've enjoyed the journey."

"Who wants coffee with their dessert?" Lily asks.

Everyone but Alyssa does.

When Lily assists Sara with bringing out the last of the desserts, she is also holding a forest green backpack.

"This is from all of us," Lily says to the room, but is looking at me. "I spoke to a friend in Finland and had him get me a list of what he thought you'd need. He said this pack would be good for your walk. There's also some equipment in there."

"Wow," I say with a huge smile. "Thanks everyone."

While eating slices of Coconut Cream Pie, Emily asks me about my trip.

"I'll be starting from the coast of The Netherlands in less than two months," I say. "I thought it would be cool to use the book I found on Lily's bookshelf to guide my way. However, the book was published in 1986, so I'll see how it goes."

After dinner, Lily herds everyone into the living room. The guitar is resting near the fireplace. Lily and I have this planned. I take the guitar and start playing the Beatles song, *Blackbird*. I don't sing, I just play. I am not confident in my singing voice, though I do occasionally sing along when I practice.

"What the hell, dude," Brody says when I finish.

He's clearly astonished. He's only known the old me; lazy and only looking for a good time. Or at least that's my guess as to how he felt during my partying days.

Next, I play, *Give a Little*, by Supertramp.

I get a round of applause and I give a slight bow.

Mary says, "I'd say your hard work has paid off."

This is the first time I've played the guitar in front of anybody other than Lily. My face starts to blush as pride washes through me. I've never been so proud of myself.

After the last of the dinner guests have left, Lily tells Brody and I, "I'm going to call it a night. I think I had too much wine." She looks tired.

We both hug her goodnight.

He and I sit in the kitchen and talk.

I think we're both tired too. Last night he and I roamed the city into the wee hours, reminiscent of our hard-partying days, but I was careful to stay in control. It felt good to hang out together. I learned that his job is stressful, and he was excited to visit so he could "decompress."

I grab two bottles of water from the fridge and set one in front of him. I open mine and take a few gulps, the chilled water refreshing.

"I'm sorry your job isn't what you'd hoped," I say.

"It's not bad, but my boss is an asshole," he says shaking his head. "He treats everyone in the department like shit."

"Why don't you quit?"

"Because the pay is good," he shrugs.

We decide to call it a night. He has an early flight, and we have a two-hour drive to O'Hare.

Brody was a big part of my life for two years, my best friend. Now I think that my feeling lost last summer had much to do with losing him from my life. He was my only *real* connection at the time; and then I had none. I *will* do a better job of reaching out to him. From our conversations, I know he could use a friendly voice to talk to.

We sometimes, encounter people, even perfect strangers, who begin to interest us at first sight, somehow suddenly, all at once, before a word has been spoken.

Fyodor Dostoyevsky, *Crime and Punishment*

EIGHT / eve

June 3 –   Amsterdam, The Netherlands

I walk off the modern light rail train that departed from the airport, my gifted pack on my back. I'm surrounded by loads of tall Dutch people, none speaking English. Layers of clouds hide the sun, but I see small patches of blue. I am swept along, as we head toward the city center. Crossing a bridge on a busy sidewalk five meters wide, then past older buildings, tidy and five stories high. I'm relieved to finally be here. Getting to Amsterdam wasn't necessarily tricky, but I was always worried about the *next* step in my journey. I have one more train ride in the morning, and then I just need to walk for well over a thousand miles to reach my destination.

My confidence in this walk being a success, meaning I finish it, is not as high as when my plane was taxiing to take off from Chicago. I have started to get nervous, mostly about my sleeping accommodations since I can't rely on a forty-year-old book. I plan on using Google to find places to stay, either campgrounds, motels, hostels, or the satellite view when I must camp in the wild. I can't plan too far ahead now, as I have no idea how far I'll be able to walk in a day. How well will my feet hold up in my new trail running shoes?

According to Google Maps, I have a nine-minute walk to my hostel, 1.8 kilometers away. Kilometers will be my new distance measurement; 1 mile equates to roughly 1.6 kms. I stop when I see an ATM and withdraw a couple hundred euros.

I feel very "solo" right now. I've not spent a lot of time alone in my life. Lonely at times, sure, but never alone. I went from my family to roommates at school and now to Lily. I have always had someone else around. How will I hold up walking by myself for the next few months?

I enter the hostel which is located next to one of the many canals running through what I'm finding is a beautiful, historic city. I hand my passport and credit card to a twenty-something girl with long dreds.

She hands me a key card and says, "This will get you into your room. You'll be in bed nine."

I find my room. It's filled with ten bunks, twenty beds. Most every bed covered in a bag or a rumpled sheet. I find mine empty, a bottom bunk, and lock up my backpack in the corresponding locker. I take a shower, followed by a nap. When evening arrives, I head out to explore.

Out of curiosity, more than anything else, I walk first to the red-light district and pass women in windows, being sure to avoid their gaze. I keep walking, turning here and there for no certain reason. Eventually, I end up at a table outside a bar sipping a Heineken. Heineken, because I passed their brewery as I walked.

I order a second and drink it slowly. I watch as people pass by on the lively streets. I look across the square to a clock tower that shows it's just after nine o'clock. I don't want to keep drinking; something I couldn't imagine thinking a year ago. After finishing my beer, I weave my way through the city streets.

Back at the hostel, I wait in line for a beer. I'm having another only because it's too early to call it a night. I look around the loud and crowded hostel and make eye contact with a cute brunette across the room. I can tell she's with three other girls, and I give a little smile. She smiles back. A second later I turn and say, "One Heineken." The same twenty-something from this afternoon pulls a long draw and hands me a sudsy beer.

I sit close to the bar at the end of one of many long communal tables. While I nurse my beer, I count the minutes until I deem it late enough, and I can go to bed. I'm excited to start my walk in the morning. I plan to get up early, take the train to The Hague, a Dutch city on the coast of the North Sea. I'll head out from the station to find someplace called Hoek van Holland, or the corner of Holland, where I will start walking. I decide, one more beer, then I'll head to bed.

Standing at the bar again, I make eye contact again with the cute girl. This time she smiles even bigger and motions with her head to come over. I smile and hold up one finger. After I get my beer, I walk over and sit beside her. Her friends are in a conversation, in French.

She says, in English, "You don't look like a backpacker."

I'm surprised she spoke in English, though a foreign accent is clear.

"What makes you think I may be one?

"Because you're here." she says. "And most others are."

"I see," I say. "Are you?"

"No, we're here to celebrate Claudia's upcoming wedding."

"Did I hear my name?" One of her friends, chimes in. She has long blonde hair and is feeling no pain.

"Hi Claudia," I say, standing and reaching over to shake her hand. "I'm Jack."

"Hi, Jack," she says with a long stare.

Then I look at the woman who invited me over and say, "Hi." I reach out to shake her hand.

"Nathalie," she says with an innocent smile.

"It's nice to meet you," I say.

Claudia asks Nathalie a question in French, and the four girls start to talk. Despite taking three years of French in high school, I don't understand what's being said.

After a minute, Nathalie says, "My friends are going to a nearby bar, but I don't feel like drinking anymore so I'm staying."

My eyes widen, and I smirk to myself, though not enough for anyone to notice.

Her friends gather their things and say to Nathalie in English, "We'll see you in the morning."

Once we're alone, Nathalie says, "You never said if you were backpacking around Europe."

"Well, until tonight I've never stayed in a hostel. But I am about to walk to the Mediterranean Sea."

"From where?"

"Here," I say, "I leave in the morning. Taking a train to the coast and then I will start out."

"How long is the walk?"

"About two thousand kilometers. I have ninety days to finish it. It's called the GR5."

"I'm familiar with the Grande Randonnée routes." French for "great trek."

"So where are you from?" I ask.

"Belgium, but I go to school in France. How about you? Are you on summer break from university?"

"Not really," I say, "I haven't been going for the last year. I flunked out. I am trying to decide what I am going to do. That's a big reason why I'm going on the walk."

"All great ideas come while walking," she says adds, "That's…"

At the same time, we say, "Nietzsche," and both give a muted laugh.

"I love that quote," I say. "And, so yeah, I am trying to figure some things out. How about you?"

"I have been studying literature but will probably change to education."

We talk a little about school, and the classes we've enjoyed. We discuss books. During our conversation she says I am to read the *Lion of Flanders*, by a Belgian author, and I assign her the book, *The Dharma Bums* by Kerouac.

Nathalie shares a few stories about her travels. Her family has always vacationed to new places around the world. To impress her, I share my adventure last summer with Brody. It makes for an entertaining story.

At a lull in the conversation, intentionally without thinking too much about it, I blurt out, "Would you like to go for a walk?"

"Yes. I would love to."

I look at the clock behind the bar, it's a quarter after eleven. I can't believe it's already that late.

We walk along canals, on cobbled streets, barely lit by old timey streetlights. As we walk further from the hostel, it gets quieter, and we find ourselves the only two around. The stars are visible above, and there is just a hint of a chill in the air.

As we walk, our conversation turns to family. Nathalie says, "My family lives in a close-knit community. I have a younger sister still at home. My dad is a carpenter, and my mom is a teacher."

"I live in a small city in the middle of the country. I have two younger brothers. My mom does hair," I say as I make the motion with my fingers as if I am cutting my hair. "My dad passed away when I was about to turn thirteen. It was sudden. An accident at home."

"I am so sorry. That's sad."

I look down at the cobbles as we walk. I stay quiet for a few seconds as the scenes from that day, once again, flash in my head: Mom running in the house screaming—my brothers and me kneeling, praying. Hours later, mom and the chaplain walking towards us—me screaming, "Why?" Because I thought I was supposed to. That night, my uncle tucking me and saying, "You're the man of the house now." The wake. After hours inside, the line of mourners running out the door; we run with our cousins, sweating. Those in line staring at *his* kids with looks that are unforgiving.

Finally, I say, "It's sad—but life goes on."

"What was your father like?"

"He was the life of any party," I say smiling. "I can only remember him smiling. He owned a barber shop and had a large circle of friends. My favorite thing was the father and son organization we belonged to. My dad, brothers, and I would go camping a few times a year with the group of over a hundred men and boys. Before he died, he was the leader of the program. Our family went from living a full and active life, to something much less."

I start to tear up and look away.

"I can't imagine."

A couple seconds pass, then she says, "Last year my parents separated, but have since reconciled. But when my mom moved out, it was tough on my sister and me. We cried a lot, not understanding why. It's still kind of awkward at home."

"That sucks," I say. "Who were you closest to, before they separated?"

"My mom," she says, with a sideways smile. "But she insisted we stay with our dad."

We share stories of other memorable times in our lives.

As we walk alongside another canal, I try, almost imperceptibly, to bump hands with her. Eventually they do, and soon join together.

We talk about my walking route, and what cities I'll be passing through. She shares her travel plans for the summer.

It's crazy what is going through my head. I've never had such a deep conversation with any girl before—not even during my many late nights at college.

Nathalie unzips a fanny pack she is wearing across her chest and takes something out. "Here, put this in."

I take the earbud, and after a second, put it in my right ear.

A song plays. It's in French and I don't understand a word, but it's beautiful.

After it ends, I ask, "Can I see your phone?"

A minute later, Ed Sheeran's *Perfect* starts playing. As we walk, our souls connect.

Eventually, we end up back near our hostel. I stop and give her hand a slight tug. She turns back with a big smile, and we move towards each other, our eyes lock, and our lips touch. Gently at first, but soon more passionately, our tongues twirling. After a minute, she pulls free, and walking backwards toward the hostel, says, "You need to get up early in the morning to start your walk."

Outside her bunk room, I lean in and whisper in her ear, "I'll stay in touch."

Once the adrenaline of meeting Nathalie subsides, thoughts turn to tomorrow and the start of my adventure. Lying in bed, the room quiet, my mind races with everything that might go wrong.

One day I will find the right words, and they will be simple.

Jack Kerouac, *The Dharma Bums*

NINE / solitude

June 10 –   Lummen, Belgium

The alarm on my phone wakes me; it's 7:00 in the morning. Light peaks through the sides of a curtain.

I am jumping ahead in my story—today is day seven of my walk, but I'll catch you up.

An alarm is something I've set only once so far. Normally, I wake with the sun, but this morning, I am sleeping in a comfortable bed in a small B&B. A long conversation with the owner kept me up late. It was the most I'd talked in a week.

Last night was only my second night staying indoors. The first was on day two, when I walked over forty kilometers to get to a hotel, already in Belgium, where I'd reserved a room. I was desperate for a hot shower, but the cost, nearly a hundred euros, was an eye-opener. At that rate, I would empty my bank account long before Nice. Since then, I've either camped in the wild or at a campground. While not free, there at least I can shower. I have also swum in a few rivers and lakes which I've found along the way, to help stay clean; my quick-drying hiking shorts doing double duty.

Today, I will keep heading towards Maastricht which is back in the weirdly shaped Netherlands. I will sleep in the woods about halfway there. Tomorrow, I plan to stop at a campground I found online. The official route then re-enters Belgium, and a few days later, the GR5 will cross into Luxembourg. My plan to walk seventy kilometers over the next two days means I will walk fewer kilometers than I've grown accustomed. So, I am okay with today's later start.

This morning I have my own bathroom and a mirror, and I get the first good look at myself in a week. Despite being outside all day, I haven't gotten the tan I expected; an overcast sky has followed me so far. I do notice sleeker cheeks under my scruffy beard. I'm starting to look more like the seventies tennis player I've been told I resemble, Bjorn Borg. I think it's the hair. I plan on growing a beard on my walk, and not cutting my hair, but I will play it by ear. I have been wearing a buff while walking to keep the sweat and hair off my face.

I put on the favorite of my two walking shirts, a gray merino wool with a picture of a mountain goat, and a lightweight, long sleeve, cream colored button up shirt, unbuttoned. It's great for the morning chill. I throw on my pack and make my way to the dining room where my hosts have my breakfast ready earlier than normal. They know I would like to get walking. They even wrap a sandwich for my lunch. I wish this friendly couple farewell and head out to begin my day.

My longest day so far, was just over fifty kilometers (or thirty-one miles), when I wild camped back-to-back nights. I walked for over sixteen hours, from dawn to dusk; my only break a two-hour nap beside a small lake. My daily mileage had been a concern before I started. My book's itinerary laid out the trip over a hundred and nine days, but my travel visa only allows me ninety. The authors recommend a total of nine rest days, so I'll need to cut those out. The good news—I've been making up ground. My long days of walking have me averaging well over forty, while the sample itinerary averages less than thirty.

My body is holding up. The only issue I've had was the straps digging into my shoulders all day. I found out later I wasn't wearing my pack correctly.

On my third day of walking, I bent my arms back over my head grasping the handle on the top of my pack to take the weight from my shoulders.

"Hallo," a man from behind me says, and then says something in a foreign language that I don't understand.

I turn to see a man with a mop of curly gray hair.

"Hello. Do you speak English?" I ask.

"Yes," he says. "Where are you from?"

We exchange why we are each here walking; he's on an afternoon stroll. Eventually the guy says, "I think you may not be using your belts properly."

"What do you mean?" I ask, confused.

He points to the belt of the pack hanging loosely around my waist. "You need to tighten that, so the weight rests on your hips."

He spends a few minutes helping me adjust the belt, and others by my chest.

"Wow," I say with a huge smile. "I can't believe the difference."

These simple adjustments give me *so* much relief.

Having already eaten breakfast at the B&B, and with lunch in my pack, I don't need to worry about food for a while. I plan to stop for dinner around six, then find a spot in the woods on the outskirts of a town, just before dusk. I estimate a thirty-eight-kilometer day.

So far on my journey I've made my way along country roads, through forest tracks, next to farmers fields, alongside canals, and on raised dykes. Wind turbines seemingly always dotting the horizon. The dominant color of my walk so far is green; the fields, the grass, the leaf covered trees, it looks and feels like early Spring back home.

My walk has taught me a lot about solitude, or maybe it's just living without distraction. Back home, when I'm with other people, I look at how they react to my actions, and I judge myself by what I assume they think. On this walk, I am gaining confidence that I have been lacking much of my life. I feel lucky to have been able to remove the many distractions in my life, yes, here, but also in the months leading up to my walk. At Lily's, it felt as though I was laying the groundwork, for what, I don't know yet. All I know is my time is better spent. My creative mind has been set free. It feels great to create things, be it music or writing, instead of always just consuming.

Ahead I spot a red and white blaze on a small concrete obelisk, signifying that my path will be turning right. All along my walk, there are signs marking the way. Sometimes it is easy to miss one of these markers, but I've managed to limit the number of wrong turns. Google Maps helps get me back on track, as well as helping me locate food.

Most of the day I walk in silence, no ear buds in. I think of things in the past, the present, the future. My mind clearing out the clutter. I walk in meditation, a thought comes, I wish it well, then send it off on a floating cloud ... I release it. But one thought sticks—Nathalie.

Before noon, my path takes me directly past a bakery. I stop. I buy a croissant which I eat immediately and a baguette for later. My time with the many shop keepers I've encountered, like just now, is fine. Pointing and smiles go a long way, but I miss out on more meaningful interactions. The language barrier, I'm told, will switch in the coming days. The north of Belgium speaks Flemish, while the south speaks French. The fact that I cannot properly communicate with all I meet has been a bit disheartening.

I have decided to try and better my situation and refresh my French. Yesterday, I downloaded a conversational French language course from my library back home. My high school French was never great; I only remembered a handful of words. When listening to my downloaded lesson, I was surprised how much came back. I listened for a couple of hours, repeating the phrases in French to the butterflies and passing birds. I plan to continue with my French lessons all along my walk.

A few hours later, I find a grassy patch alongside a small stream. I take off my shoes and socks, remove my sweaty buff, and lean back against my pack. I unwrap the sandwich to find ham and cheese on a small baguette and grab my water.

I've thought about my dad a lot on my walk, and often talk to him out loud. I always have. The most common place is the golf course, a place where we connected one on one.

Back home, when I talk to him, it's usually either asking for help—or forgiveness.

Today, I think about my rudderless years, and ask, "Who might I have become, with him here?"

Before I leave, I fill my water bottle from the stream and filter it with my ultraviolet wand.

The rest of the afternoon I walk at my typical good clip, and the kilometers tick by. After my language lesson, I start listening to an entertaining book that was recommended by the library app on my phone, *The Unlikely Pilgrimage of Harold Fry*. I am enjoying this simple story of an old man's spur-of-the-moment walk across England. It's a simple read, or should I say listen.

At the beginning of my walk, I was nervous about finding a place to sleep each night, but I am no longer sweating this part of my journey. Finding a place to simply lie down for the night is not usually tricky. My bivy sack has been a must; it keeps my sleeping bag dry from rain and the morning dew, and it's saved me from having to find a bed every night. My bivy was tested on day four when rain poured in the middle of the night. I stayed dry. It passed the test. This cost-saving, coupled with my food costs being minimal, (thanks to an ever-present baguette) I'm finding my bank account still intact. Another area of improvement after a week on the road, I'm no longer shy about knocking on a stranger's door and asking to fill my water bottle when the need arises.

Walking all day under the sky, be it blue or a misty haze, simply being outside, breathing in the fresh air, my body ever moving—this is how life is meant to be. I have only what I need.

The opening of the Walt Whitman poem, *Song of the Open Road*, perfectly fits where my mind is this afternoon. "Healthy, free, the world before me. The long brown path before me leading me wherever I choose..."

I enter the town of Bilzen at a little past 6:00 pm, unsure of what I will eat for dinner. Most nights, I'll use packaged meat and cheese to make a sandwich. Tonight, however, I am not feeling it. When I unexpectedly pass a sushi restaurant, my mind is made up. I enter, conscious of my atypical dress, and odor, though *I* can't smell it. The meal is delicious, but my eyes were bigger than my stomach. My hunger on this walk has not been what I'd expected. I'm rarely famished after a long day's walk; my hunger is quashed with a small evening meal. I need just enough to fuel my daily exertions.

While trying to clear my plate, I use the satellite view on my phone and find a patch of trees a few kilometers ahead. It's just after eight when I leave the restaurant, so I still have two hours of daylight. I wander around this small town and find a bench to sit and people-watch. When I see a family walk by, eating what I think is gelato, I set out on a new quest. I walk up and down nearby streets until I find the gelato shop. I order a combination of strawberry and chocolate in a dish, then find a seat outside. I eat my treat, smiling, thinking of my life on the road.

When I finish, I stand to toss my dish in a garbage can near the door. I feel a twinge on the side of my right foot. I hadn't felt that before. I take a few steps and the twinge remains. It's not exactly painful, but I feel *something* with each step. I'm sure it will go away eventually. I toss on my pack and head towards the path that will lead me out of the city. The feeling remains, and my gait changes as I try to reduce the weight I put on the outside of my foot. I continue at *almost* my normal pace. I had planned to walk a bit further tonight, but I stop at the first grove of trees I deem stealthy enough.

It's not dark yet, but I want to stay off my foot. I get my sleeping situation settled, then, like most evenings, I sit on a fallen tree and speak aloud into the Notes app on my small iPhone SE. I record what runs through my mind and what I experienced on my walk today.

As I lie in bed, bathed in a dusky light, my mind races with what the twinge might mean. I convince myself a night's rest is all it needs.

Harold could no longer pass a stranger without acknowledging the truth that everyone was the same, and also unique; and that this was the dilemma of being human.

Rachel Joyce, *The Unlikely Pilgrimage of Harold Fry*

TEN / detour

June 11 –   Bilzen, Belgium

I lie in my bivy, afraid to stand. I make circles with my ankle, testing to see if I feel anything bad. I don't, but I still have a feeling of dread.

I find my headlamp near my makeshift pillow, a packing cube filled with my clothes. I switch it on; the forest comes alive. I scoot out of my sleeping bag and slowly stand.

I feel a tightness in my foot, and when I step, the twinge is still there. Fuck!

I can walk fine, but clearly there is something wrong. My mind races, trying to decide what I should do. The first thing is to get out of the woods. I pack up quickly and make my way to the pavement that runs next to the trees.

Now I want to find a comfortable place to sit and think. I walk, putting my weight on the inside of my foot, but the twinge is still there. I google "foot pain," then "a twinge on the outside of my foot." I find nothing reassuring, just a list of possible problems.

Heading east, I watch as the sun peaks above the horizon, the sky brightens as I walk along a street through a commercial area, not yet open for the day. I see a bus stop with a bench up ahead and head there.

I sit and try to come up with a plan. Until finding this stop, I hadn't thought of a bus. Now I hope for an early one to Maastricht. My plan *was* for the campground tonight, south of the biggest city yet along my route. If I hop on a bus, I can jump maybe fifteen kilometers ahead, and then rest my foot. At first glance, I think I'm in luck, the timetable shows a stop here in twenty minutes. I smile and let out my breath.

My relief is short lived. Upon closer inspection, I find the bus runs here only on weekdays; today is Sunday—fuck, fuck, fuck.

I look at the map I tore out of my book, then I check Google Maps, to find the straightest shot to my destination. I will head there and then decide.

I walk on, feeling it with each step. I slow my pace, thinking I have been pushing too hard. Maybe with my mileage and the extra weight of my pack, my body is telling me to slow, or maybe even to stop.

My mind races with what stopping would mean. My goal is to walk the whole way, and to prove to myself I can complete something big; plus, I am loving the adventure and *want* to keep going. I think of everyone back home who I told about my trip; stopping now—what would they think?

I'd feel like a failure, coming up short again.

I put in my earbuds and play two songs on repeat, Pink's *F**kin Perfect* and Eminem's *Lose Yourself*, both songs that give me inspiration.

The kilometers tick by slowly. I stop for food but keep walking, wanting only to get to Maastricht as soon as I can. The twinge seems to worsen, or maybe it's just in my head. After four hours I cross the border, which lies just outside the big city. I check Google Maps and set my course for a large green space in the city's center.

Sitting in the grass, I eat a lunch of croquettes and fries. My planned for campground is twenty kilometers away. I can still walk, but I know it isn't helping. It's now clear I can't keep walking all day, every day; I should stop, or at least pause my adventure.

What do I do now? I am *not* going to walk to the campground. It's only 11:30 am, so I have time to decide.

If I must end my walk, so be it. I've not bought a return ticket, so I can fly home whenever I want. I decide to find a hostel or cheap hotel and rest a few days, hoping my foot heals.

I find a hostel on Google; it's close, only two-minutes away. But, since it's still early, I'll stay here in the park, relax, and lie in the sun.

If this *is* the end—what can I do in Europe before I fly home? I run through the big cities and when I hit on Paris, I stop. Using the *Rome2Rio* app on my phone, I find I can get there in three hours and forty-seven minutes. The train station is only a ten-minute walk away, and the next train leaves in thirty minutes. I throw on my pack and go. Decision made.

***

I walk out of the Félix Faure Metro stop and walk a block to the Three Ducks Hostel. While on the train, I'd reserved a bed for the next three nights. I check in and find my bed. It's only 6:30 pm.

I find it funny that no one I know has a clue where I am. I lie in my bunk and check the price of a plane ticket home, but I'm not going to book anything yet. My plan is to take public transportation around the city for the next couple of days and see the sights.

I am not tired, having napped on the train. I shower, change into the cleanest shirt I have, and head down to the bar. While I drink a beer I start talking with a Canadian guy, Mick. He shares stories of his travels around Europe; he's been backpacking by train for the last six weeks. We are soon joined by three more solo travelers, most about my age, but Christy, another American, is at least twenty years older. The night passes as the five of us drink round after round. When two of our newly formed crew head to bed, Mick says, "Who wants to go to the Eiffel Tower?"

"I'm in," I say.

"Me too," Christy says.

The three of us leave the hostel, our destination only a fifteen-minute walk. The twinge is still there. I was planning to limit my walking, but I couldn't say no to seeing the icon lit up. Three "large" beers have me feeling good, and my foot issue fades to the back of my mind. The three of us laugh all the way there. Mick wants to go up in the tower, but it's too late, the ticket booth is closed. We walk around the base, then find an excellent vantage point to sit. A street vendor walks by with a cooler full of beer, only two euros each. I buy three, and share.

"We have to wait until the hour turns," Mick tells us. "You'll be glad we did."

The three of us continue telling stories from our lives as a woman plays a violin just a few feet away.

Soon, the tower, which was already lit up, starts to sparkle. My jaw drops.

I think back to where my day started, and smile. Now, I'm in Paris, with new friends, watching this breathtaking sight. It's funny how things sometimes work out.

The next two days, I take it easy. I ride the Metro all around the city but limit my walking to a minimum while still taking in the sights. On my last night, I am back in the bar talking to someone I just met. A short time later, we head out for dinner at a restaurant just down the street. We talk about our lives, and I tell him about my journey.

"I had to stop when my foot started acting up. That's the only reason I'm here."

"So, what are you going to do?"

"I am going to give it a try. I'm taking the train back to where I left off and will start walking again tomorrow." I am nervous, but I feel I should at least try to finish what I started.

ELEVEN / breathe

June 14 –   Vielsalm, Belgium

Rhythmic clacking and chatter fill the air as the French countryside flashes by and I think about my days in Paris. While I liked seeing the city, it was the time I spent with those I met in the hostel, other solo travelers from around the world, that I really enjoyed. That is a part of travel I had not yet experienced, except for those few magical hours on my first night in Europe.

The clack, clack, clack of the train continues, as I head to Vielsalm, Belgium, about three days further along the GR5 than where I left off. Last night, while lying in bed, I looked carefully at the calendar and a map to come up with this plan. I will slow my pace, and not do anything stupid to aggravate my foot. It has been improving since my first full day in Paris. I was careful not to walk too much, and the fact that I wasn't carrying my pack for those few days helped even more. I have reduced my pack weight; tossing my guidebook after taking pictures of each page; and I gave up on a solar power bank that didn't work as well as I'd hoped. There is nothing else in my bag I feel I can do without.

The train pulls into the station, just after 1:00 pm. I step gingerly from the train, my pack now back on. My foot feels okay. What I feel is a tightness, no longer a twinge. I walk slowly as I make my way back to the official route. My plan today is to walk about sixteen kilometers, stopping often as I make my way. I will gradually build my distance travelled in the days and (hopefully) weeks to come.

Four hours later, I've covered my planned distance, but it's early and my foot still feels good. I set my sights on the town of Burg-Reuland, another six kilometers ahead.

Soon, I reach a beautiful lake along my route, the perfect place for a mid-afternoon break. I eat a sandwich I picked up from a boulangerie near the train station, while I rest against my pack. This scene, a small lake next to a large oak tree, reminds me of the spot my dad used to take my brothers and I fishing. I smile at the memory. Then I remember the last time we were there. It was the week before he died.

The question I've thought of only a few times since that fateful day, now pops into my head. The one I'm afraid to answer. Today, there's nothing to distract me—no tv to turn on, no booze or drug to numb my mind. It's just me and *this* question.

Why wasn't I still with him, helping, on his final day? I was the oldest son. Why wasn't I there?

I try to piece the events of that day together.

At some point, I must have asked, "Can I go now?" And he replied, "Yes." Though I don't remember this.

Was I being lazy or was there some show I wanted to watch?

The reason doesn't matter. The only thing that does … he was alone when a live wire fell … and no one was there to help.

Tears start to fall. I speak the words "I'm sorry" and beg for his forgiveness.

I break down. I ugly cry, sobbing while still trying to hold back.

Again, I say out loud, "Dad … I'm sorry."

I stay under this tree for the next hour as I start the work of forgiving myself.

An hour later, I walk into a small hotel. The woman behind the desk says, "Guten Abend." This village is in a German speaking region of Belgium, very near the German border. Luxembourg, too, is only a day's walk from here.

In the morning, I resume my normal routine; up early, walk for an hour, then stop and eat. I keep my pace slow. I cross the border into Luxembourg and am soon walking on a beautiful forest track. Occasionally I catch a peek through the trees of the Cur River below, Germany on the opposite bank.

In the early afternoon, I check my phone for a place to stay near the town of Dasbourg-Pont, the stopping point recommended in my book. I could easily stay the night in the trees, but I'm happy when I find a hostel close.

My route follows the river for the next few hours and I don't see another soul. This area is remote and there is no food to be found. I've already finished what I had left in my pack—bread and a half a bag of chips. Luckily, I find water in a gently flowing stream. I drink my fill and leave with my bottle full.

I am famished when I finally arrive at what the map says is my target. But I find only a gas station and a bridge. I read the section of my book more carefully and find this was a border crossing station, now, no longer in use. There is no town, just the bridge. My hostel is across the river, only a few hundred meters away. I check in, shower, and find something to eat.

My return to the trail has been a success. I've walked almost fifty kilometers in the last two days, and my foot is back to normal. I feel relieved. My brush with defeat, having my walk almost end, has increased my willingness to spend a little more for comfort. Before, I had been concerned with watching every penny, trying to make this adventure as inexpensive as I could. Now, money is no longer my most important consideration.

Before bed, I spend a few minutes thinking, reflecting on the day and where my mind has been. Many days I've had some good insights, some even worthy of an index card. My favorite today—'Solitude, I'm finding, is a must to connect to yourself. And what's more important than that?'

TWELVE / stars

June 23 –   Château du Landsberg - Vosges Mountains, France

It's been over a week since I last checked in. I'm now in France. Things are going according to plan, and I'm happy to report, I haven't had any more issues with my foot. The mountains have been the biggest change, as my distance covered each day is down and my calorie burn is *way* up.

Today has been typical of my trek through the Vosges (it rhymes with rose) Mountains, with many ups and downs. Finding food has been a challenge, as there are far fewer villages in the mountains. It's after 8:00 pm, with thirty-four kilometers already in the books. I should stop soon and eat what's left in my pack.

I stumble upon *this* place an hour before dark. An ancient Château abandoned in a small clearing—only steps off my forest path. The walls crumbling, the roof long gone, but the bulk remains. I stop here for tonight. How could I not? I rest against an inside wall and finish my baguette and the remainder of my cheese. My legs, though stronger now, are beat and need to rest. Setting up camp takes only a minute; I roll out my bivy, insert my sleeping pad and bag; I brush my teeth, then crawl inside. I'm asleep long before dark.

I wake in the middle of the night. I look up to a sky brimming with the brightest stars I've ever seen. It is silent, *here*, inside the walls of this old stone home. My heart begins to race. My mouth hangs open. My head starts to tingle, and then my body. My lips turn, and my smile expands.

I awake, again, before the sun. Headlamp on, I roll up my bivy, put my sleeping bag in its little stuff sack, fold my sleeping pad accordion style, and pack up. I grab my toothbrush from the top compartment of my bag, brush, then down what water I have left. I throw on my pack and walk quietly out of my abandoned castle in the middle of the woods and resume my walk, still amazed by my moment of ecstasy last night. It was surreal, and the only time in my life I've had a feeling like that. I try to find some meaning in it, but all I can think is … it's the universe telling me I'm on the right path.

On this trip I am learning what quotes like "Be here now" and "Live in the moment" actually mean. After the first weeks on the trail, I've seldom thought of the past, or my future; that only leaves "now." Being focused on the moment—I *am* here now.

I have been waiting for an epiphany to direct me to my life's path. But maybe it's as simple as learning what it means to live in the now, and if I'm lucky, to stumble upon more moments like last night when the universe embraced my body and mind.

Moving all day feels great, but so do my leisurely rest breaks in the afternoons. Seeing the progress on the map is exciting, but not in an "Are we there yet?" way. My priority this morning is finding food. As the sun starts its climb, I place my headlamp into a pocket on my pack. On goes my buff, my forehead already damp with sweat.

I've started having more extended interactions when walking through towns. My efforts to try and speak French have made a big difference. I now look forward to walking into a shop and asking for what I need. Normally, I will translate my opening sentence using my translation app, quietly repeating the translation before I walk in.

A few days ago, I tried to learn something from everyone I met. I'd ask a question, even if it was just directions to the nearest patisserie. I only spoke French, though I used Google Translate more than ever. My questions led to a valuable discovery; drinkable water can be found in every cemetery. It's the law. It was a good day and led to more smiles and laughs than any yet on my walk. I'm still listening to my language course for at least a part of each day.

On a diet that consists primarily of bread and cheese, I am losing weight. I will occasionally eat a meal at a restaurant at midday if I am near a town, the same goes for dinner, but most days, that is not the case. I have Lily to thank for my shorts staying up, as she insisted I bring a belt. I can now measure my walk by the number of new holes I have to punch.

Nearing the town of Heiligenstein, under an early morning sky I find a grocery store on the map. The store is over a kilometer off my route and adds to my total distance walked. This is not an uncommon occurrence. I'm still walking long days, though, like I said, the ground I cover is less in the mountains. However, last week I had a "zero day" where I didn't walk at all.

One night, over dinner at my gîte (a French B&B) near the town of Nancy, I learned that my host, Marceline, in her seventies, was looking for someone to do a few minor repairs. I told her I may be able to help. Together, we walk around her house and she points out what needs fixing; a railing needs repair, a leaky faucet needs to be replaced, and a bedroom door that won't shut.

"Oui. Je peux les réparer," I say. I can fix these.

In the morning, Marceline takes me to a not very well-lit basement with a dirt floor and shows me an old work bench covered in tools. Then on Google Maps, she shows me where the hardware store is. I spend the morning and afternoon on these little projects, while

Marceline keeps bringing me food and drink. Afterwards, I shower and then we enjoy dinner with another guest that arrived late in the day. In the morning, she hands me a fifty euro note and a packed lunch. We share smiles and a big hug. I wear that smile on my face for the rest of the morning.

Gîtes have been my preferred accommodation since crossing into France. It's worked out that I can find one about every other day with my mileage requirements. I enjoy interacting with my hosts, usually an older woman but a younger couple with a toddler hosted me one night. They spoke English, and we had a long conversation over a delicious dinner.

The kindness I have received along my walk has been a surprise. From big smiles, to food and drink offers from locals as I walk through their village or town, to the generosity of my evening hosts I thought there must be something about a solo hiker with just a pack on his or her back. Eventually, however, I decide maybe it's not the pack, it's just people taking the opportunity to practice kindness whenever a situation arises.

It's amazing how excited *I* get whenever I have the chance to be kind with those I meet, even if it's just a nod and a smile. But, remembering to always be kind is not easy. Sometimes I forget, that's why *I* must practice.

There was a situation last year, one that still eats at me. I was standing in the checkout line at a discount store; a mom and her son were in front of me being rung up. I watched as the mom realized she didn't have enough cash to cover her purchase.

"We can't get the notebook binder," she tells her son. "I don't have enough money."

Her son nods and says, "It's okay mom." But I see tears welling in his eyes. It was early in the morning on a late August day, and I was just stuck behind a bus with its red flashing lights. She also had pencils, paper, and glue on the conveyer belt … so, I knew they were headed to his first day of school. I felt bad for them. I had more than enough in my pocket to cover the difference. I thought about offering to help, but was afraid to, thinking the woman might take offense. I remained silent. Now, a year later, this memory still sticks in my head; wishing I could go back in time, to at least make the offer; thinking now, she would have welcomed the help.

It's been hours since my resupply stop when I enter a small village. I pass by a boulangerie, hesitate, but keep walking. I have lunch in my pack. A minute later, I turn around. My baguette can wait. I want to practice my French.

"Bonjour, Madame," I say to the middle-aged woman behind the glass counter.

"Bonjour, Monsieur. Ca va," she says with a slight smile.

"Je vais bien," I respond." Je voudrais la quiche et le croissant s'il vous plaît."

"Oui," she says as she opens the back of the counter, wraps each in bakery paper, and puts them in a small bag. "Ce sera quatre euros."

I hand her a five euro note. She hands me a one-euro coin in return.

"Merci, beaucoup," I say with a smile. "Passe une bonne journée." Have a nice day.

A smile washes across her face.

I eat my croissant as soon as I walk out the door then resume my walk. The temperature has been climbing and I'm feeling it, and it's not even noon. I want to stop but keep walking until I find a spot in the shade to take my afternoon break. Finally, I find a place, a small patch of grass under a tree, just off the gravel path. I throw off my pack, take off my shoes and socks — relief. I eat my small quiche and down a half liter of Aquarius (a Gatorade like drink) before laying in the grass, my head resting on one of my shoes. I watch birds fly overhead; one finds a perch in my tree. She tweets her greeting, or maybe she's asking for part of my lunch.

For the first time, I feel a deep connection to nature. I've never really paid close attention to my surroundings outdoors. Here on my walk, I've started to listen. The sounds of animals moving in the woods before I fall asleep, the birds chirping greetings in the morning light— I love it all. Being outside in all kinds of weather and at all times of day has sometimes been challenging, but it's made this walk feel like a real adventure.

I'm unsure if I fall asleep, but my eyes remain closed for at least an hour. Feeling refreshed, I pack up and resume.

I have yet to meet any fellow long-distance hikers on my solo journey. I've seen a woman's name in the guestbook at two separate gîtes. I've found out that she is also walking the GR5. She was two days ahead of me at the first gîte, and one day ahead at the second. I hope to catch up with her at some point. I am realizing, firsthand, that humans are social animals, and we crave connections with others.

Listening to *Wild*, my latest audiobook, I find it a perfect adventure story to accompany me on mine. The hours pass quickly. I stop only to fill my water bottle when an opportunity appears.

Today, I must reach the town of Ribeauvillé where I have a bed reserved. It's thirty-eight kilometers from last night's castle in the woods. I will need to maintain a faster than average pace to get there before 6:00 pm when the host told me dinner will be served. The hottest temperature usually hits around 3:00 pm, and today is no exception. I long ago sweat through my shirt and I now pour water over my head a couple of times to keep from overheating. I think about my foot since I've been pushing, but my pace remains.

I find my chamber d'hôte, another name for a gîte, and knock on the door thirty minutes before six.

"Hello, you must be Jack," says a youngish guy in perfect English. He looks to be in his early thirties. "I am Francois, my wife, Brigitte, is in the kitchen preparing dinner. Let me show you to your room."

He leads me to the second floor, pointing out the bathroom. He opens a door, inside a single bed, an armoire, and a small desk. "Dinner will be served at six," he says, then turns to go.

After a shower, I wash my walking clothes and hang them to dry in the armoire. I change into my clean "town clothes" and head downstairs.

"Bonsoir," says Brigitte.

"Bonsoir," I reply.

I sit at a table that seats eight, next to an older gentleman and across from a woman who I find is his wife. Also at the table is a middle-aged man wearing a shirt and tie. The common language at the table is, of course, French. Though everyone speaks at least some English. Tonight I will try to speak only French. It will be a good test.

Over our three-course meal, we all share stories. I talk about my walk, though I find myself speaking English more than French, not wanting to slow the conversation. The food is delicious, and the entire evening a joy. After the table is cleared, everyone moves to the formal living room. Francois brings out a tray with six glasses and Brigitte joins us a couple minutes later.

Looking out doors that lead to a large deck, I see the colors of the sky starting to turn.

"I'm going to watch the sunset from your deck, if that is okay?" I say to Francois.

"Great idea!" he says. "I'll invite the others."

The six of us, freshly poured glasses of wine in hand, sit around a large table on the deck and toast to "une belle nuit,"

I have enjoyed the sunset *almost* every night along my walk. I have made a point of it. Most mornings, I can watch the sun rise, but it's watching the sun set over a new horizon that really makes me smile.

As I lay in bed tonight, I think about the choices I've made in my life. In the past I questioned most of them, but tonight I realize somewhere along the way I have made a right turn, one that led me here.

I'm a free spirit who never had the balls to be free.

Cheryl Strayed, *Wild*

THIRTEEN / interlude

June 28 –   Bruges, Belgium

A few days later, I am sitting in a large room decorated with streamers; two large balloons float above one of several large tables, one an eight and the other a zero. The windows look out to an empty courtyard and a golden hour light.

The gentleman next to me stands and starts to speak to the twenty or so gathered. He says something in Flemish, which, to my inexperienced ear, still sounds like indiscernible gibberish. He raises his glass and says, "Santé." We all raise our glasses and repeat his toast.

Nathalie, seated on my other side, tells me, "He wished Ella a happy eightieth birthday."

Everyone is gathered here in what Nathalie calls the "Common House." Ella, a spry eighty, shares her gratitude with those here — more with her face and her gestures than in words.

"She is like a grandmother to me," Nathalie tells me. "This was a big one; I would not have missed it."

I'm as surprised as you that I'm back in Belgium.

In a text last week, Nathalie said, "I've been thinking of you."

By that point, she'd started to fade from my mind, as the dream of a relationship grew increasingly unlikely. Her text came out of the blue. My initial thought was, "I can't spare the days. I won't be able to finish." After crunching the numbers, I decided I could afford to take a few days off. From that moment, the excitement had been building to see her again. I couldn't wait to see her smile, her full crimson lips.

Yesterday morning, I walked to the closest station, hopped on one train, and then another. As my train got closer, my heart began to race. My mind returned to our one encounter—her eyes—our connection was real.

My train pulls in a little past 9:00 pm. Nathalie is on the platform to greet me with a long hug. We melt into one another. Her first words, "I like the beard."

We stroll together hand in hand, as the sun sets behind us. It's about an hour walk to her home, where I meet her parents and sister. We talk and laugh much of the time, and even manage a kiss or two. Eventually, we leave her family's home, and she walks me to my room back in the large house that her community shares. I lay in bed, thinking myself an idiot for even considering *not* coming to see her.

Before heading to this party tonight, I down a beer; the social lubricant I still feel I need. When we get to dinner, I eagerly accept the offer of another. I am not sure why, as everyone here has been so engaging.

In Amsterdam, when Nathalie told me she lived in a "close-knit" community, I didn't know what she meant. When we got here last night, she took me into her family's place; an apartment in a small cluster of similar size buildings alongside the large "Common House". I've learned each of the similar buildings is comprised of either three or four homes. No cars are allowed but a parking lot sits just outside the tightly packed community. All of this in the middle of a city. Nathalie tells me, "Everyone owns their unit, and we share the common spaces."

In the twenty-four hours I've been here, I get a different vibe. It reminds me of being back on staff at my old summer camp, no campers, just the staff hanging out.

Like most everyone else here, Julian, the guy next to me, speaks perfect English. I share with him who I am and why I am here.

He listens intently, asks follow-up questions, probing. He tells me he is one of the founders of this place and says they "live intentionally." Julian tells me he met two other original members at a conference years ago. He tells me, "This is our shared dream."

"I like it," I say. "It's different."

"My wife and kids are at the lake this weekend," he says. "It's too bad. They would have loved to meet a friend of Nathalie's. My daughters are sixteen and fourteen, and they idolize her."

Our dinner tonight has been prepared by two residents, their gift to Ella. Our plates are set before us by three kids, no older than twelve. On my plate, ten or so mussels, and a mound of frites, or French fries.

Nathalie's fifteen-year-old sister, Lara, asks me, "What has been your favorite part of your trek?"

"The sense of adventure," I say. "It's something new for me."

"It sounds fun," Lara says.

"Yeah, it is. It's been a solitary trip for sure. But I love it!"

I learn how to eat the mussels by watching those around me.

Using the hinged shell of one of the mussels like tweezers, I remove the meat and drop it into my mouth.

The texture is firmer than I expect. I can't immediately identify the taste, but it's a little like a clam.

"It has the taste of the ocean," Julian says.

He's right. It has a salty taste, but also the mild taste of a mushroom and a hint of sweetness. An interesting mix of the earth and sea.

Sitting across from me, Nathalie's mom tells me about the education system in Belgium. She is an elementary school teacher in town. I share some differences compared to my public education in the states. I make no mention of my higher education experience.

Dinner is delicious, and the feel of this evening is reminiscent of the church "potlucks" of years past. I learn this community eats together twice a week, with "over 90% participation." Anything not on one of the dinner nights are "special happenings," like tonight.

While eating dessert, an "appelflap," (or apple turnover) I gently tap Nathalie's knee to let her know I'm thinking of her, while I continue my conversation with Julian.

After dinner, we join a small group of her friends in a room just off the dining area. There's a piano and a couple of brass instruments, including a saxophone. I smile when I spot an acoustic guitar in the corner. There is a huge beat-up leather sectional and a few chairs lined up against two walls. One of her friends plays the piano while another sings *Imagine*. It's beautiful. Then, a guy plays a slow jazz song on the sax. One of them asks if I play an instrument.

"The guitar," I say. "I'd love to play something."

I grab the guitar and sit on the nearest chair.

As I play the song, *Banana Pancakes*, I look up to astonishment on Nathalie's face.

After our impromptu music session, Nathalie and I walk past another small room. She says, "That's where Ella taught me to throw pottery."

I hold open the door to the central courtyard, the sky now black, and ask Nathalie, "How long have you known her?"

"Ten years," she says, "she was here for the opening."

The two of us go for a walk under the stars. We stroll through the surrounding neighborhood, talking seriously. We make it back to the Common House and head upstairs to the spare room; the same one I slept alone in last night. I open the door; she walks in, and I follow. She turns and locks the door.

Act as if what you do makes a difference. It does.
– William James

A framed quote in the Common House.
Translated by Nathalie.

FOURTEEN / climb

July 1 –   Pontarlier, France

I'm just finishing the second full day of walking since my four days off trail. I resumed in the same town where I'd hopped the train to get to Nathalie's.

After our time together, it's not likely she'll fade from my thoughts. It was a perfect weekend—in every possible way, but it was just a one-time fling. Before we said our final goodbye on the train platform, it was agreed that a long-distance "thing" was not in the cards. Friends …we shall be. Still, it was hard to say goodbye.

I reach the city of Pontarlier just before 5:00 pm and navigate to tonight's accommodation, the Auberge de Jeunesse, or youth hostel. I desperately need a shower, having slept in the wild the last two nights. I've been walking non-stop for almost twelve hours, focused on getting here tonight. Pontarlier is one of the larger cities along my route. I want to explore the city tomorrow morning, start walking in the early afternoon, then walk until dark.

Checking in, I pay my twenty-five euros and find my assigned bed. The hot water feels amazing as I wash my hair, a tangled mess. I need to get some conditioner. I didn't bring any, not wanting to carry the extra weight. I dry off and look into a steamy mirror, surprised by my appearance. I'd felt the weight loss in my waist, evidenced by a recent hole punch. I notice the difference even more when I walk naked, I mean, without my pack. I feel lighter on my feet. I have a surprisingly full beard, a dark tan, and my cheeks look even thinner. I touch my face as I look side to side. I originally planned on growing my beard for my entire walk, but it's starting to get uncomfortable, at least the mustache hanging over my lip.

I put on my town clothes which I haven't worn in three days. They are now a bit wrinkled. I slip on my sandals and head to the kitchen to fill my water bottle.

A tall man with a thick head of gray hair and a face creased with deep wrinkles, approaches.

"I saw you come in with your pack. Are you walking the Via Francigena (pronounced Fran·**Chee**·Gena, the emphasis on the Chee)?"

"No," I say, "I'm on the GR5. I'm walking to Nice." Thinking he would be impressed. "What is the Via Francigena?" I ask.

"It's a pilgrimage to Rome."

"Rome!" I say with a shocked expression. "How far is that from here?"

"Another two months, give or take."

"When—and where did you start?"

"I started from my home in the Netherlands about four weeks ago."

"Wow! That's so cool."

"Why don't we have a seat? I'm waiting on Tracy, who is also walking the Via. We're headed to a store to do some shopping and get dinner."

We take seats at an empty table in the dining area.

"So, how about you?" he asks. "Where did you start out?"

"Near Amsterdam. At the Hook of Holland," I say, forgetting the Dutch term. "That's where my book told me the route started."

"I live not too far away; I live in Eindhoven. I headed south and met up with the Francigena in Reims."

"Is Tracy your wife?" I inquire. "Or a friend from back home?"

He laughs. "No, we met about a week ago along the trail. We've stayed at the same place a few times and have gotten to know one another. She's from Australia."

Damn, I think, she's come a long way to walk here.

Tracy, a middle-aged woman with dark, curly hair approaches wearing flip-flops and a smile.

"That feels much better," she says, her Australian accent obvious, her hair still wet from her shower.

"This is ..." the man starts to say, before realizing we haven't exchanged names.

"Jack," I say reaching out my hand to Tracy. "Hi Tracy," I say with a smile.

"Cor," he says. "It's always nice to meet a fellow pilgrim."

We shake hands. I like the fact that he called me a "pilgrim," as if I am also on a pilgrimage of sorts.

"Would you like to join us?" Cor asks.

"That would be great," I say, excited to meet my first fellow hikers.

The three of us walk side by side on a wide sidewalk next to the main thoroughfare in town, heading away from the town center. We each share a little of our story as we walk. Tracy started her walk from Canterbury, England. She walked to the coast, took a ferry across the English Channel to Calais, and is now walking to Rome. Like me, she has three months to get to her destination. Cor, living in the European Union, has no time constraint; residents in any of the member countries are free to travel, work, or live in any of the E.U. countries.

The two "pilgrims" tell me about their route. Soon they will be walking through Switzerland, crossing the Alps, and then through Italy, including a stretch through Tuscany and into Rome. I get a bit jealous. Their journey sounds more interesting than mine, which remains in France. My walk has been amazing, but not terribly scenic so far.

"I'm walking the GR5 because I found a thirty-year-old book that detailed this route, and it sounded exciting. I didn't know about your walk."

As we move, I can't help but notice Cor's calves. They are almost as thick as my thighs. He tells me he has done several long walks throughout his life, but this one may be his last. He's sixty-eight but clearly still fit. The reason, he says, "My partner doesn't like me being gone for months at a time. She doesn't like being alone. She likes to hike, but not like this."

Tracy tells me, "This is my first long walk, and I've been planning it for years. My government job allows employees to take six months off every ten years, that is, if they choose."

"I didn't know what to expect. I glanced through my book and looked at a few backpacking blogs. But I am finding I love it. It's such a simple life. Walk, eat, sleep. Repeat."

"You could always start heading to Rome in the morning," Tracy says with a shrug.

"I don't know anything about the Francigena," I say, my brain turning over the possibility. "I don't think I have time anyways."

"When does your visa expire?"

"August 30th."

"Mine's up ten days after yours," Tracy says. "I think you can make it. If not, you can take a train and skip a boring part."

"I'll think about it," I say, already leaning towards changing my destination. The idea of walking with others is appealing; I don't think many people are walking the GR5.

The three of us wander through a store as large as any Walmart, the Hyper U. I pick up some necessities and a battery-operated hair trimmer to tame my mustache and beard. We eat dinner in the food court inside this massive store before our saunter back. I stop for a few seconds to look back at the setting sun.

I listen to myself.

I text my mom and Lily while lying in bed in the morning. "I'm headed to Rome."

I had set out on this journey to walk to Nice, and for a moment it feels as though I'm not following through on my plan. Failing to follow through … something I've always done. But this feels different, I am simply changing course. I can't pass up the opportunity—it is *my* journey after all. Like my course change when I moved to Madison, I don't know if it's the right choice, but I must live with it.

After researching the walk last night, I think I can make it in time. Tracy helped me download an app and GPS tracks to my phone, so I now have a map with a blue line all the way to Rome. She also shared images of a spreadsheet listing all the places to stay, and even gave me what she says is a "Pilgrim's Passport."

"You'll need one to stay at the many pilgrim-only accommodations. I carried an extra, just in case."

It sounds like life as a "pilgrim" on the road to the Vatican will be easy logistically, but more challenging physically, having to hike through several mountain ranges along the way. While I never lost the enthusiasm for my walk to Nice, I must admit, I feel a renewed excitement about making the change.

The three of us start out together just as the sky begins to brighten. We share more stories as we make our way; our pace slower than mine was solo. Just before noon we reach Switzerland. Our path crosses the border in the middle of a forest. We walk next to an old guard booth. A short, barbed wire fence runs into the woods in both directions, a wooden gate stands open; there is not another soul here.

One great thing about the Western European countries forming their "Union" is that border crossings with member countries are no longer a thing. However, I wish I could get a passport stamp from each country I travel through. I find it odd, there is not even a sign that says, "Welcome to Switzerland." But our GPS clearly shows we've just crossed the almost invisible border.

We continue in a line, along a narrow dirt path through the trees. I'm excited to be in yet another country. I've been in five countries in the last month (six if you count my one night in Germany), this after never having left the U.S. in my first twenty years.

With the list of accommodations provided by Tracy, I am looking forward to the fact that I likely won't need to camp again. As we walk, I tell them about my nights in the wild. They are surprised, as they have found beds every night. "I don't mind sleeping outside, but I do prefer a cheap bed."

Cor warns me, "There will be places to stay, but the cost of lodging will be much higher in Switzerland."

Tonight, the three of us will be staying at a chamber d'hôte in the town of Lingerolle. A bed in the "dortoir" (or dorm) and dinner will run more than double what I have been paying.

It turns out to be well worth the cost. As we dine on the patio, the town's clock towers over our table. There is a chill, but the wine (included with dinner) warms me. It's a beautiful night here under a starry sky. There are twelve of us around the table, including our hosts. The discussion centers on what brought each of us here; we three are the only ones on a trek, the other guests are all on holiday.

Lying in bed tonight, I'm grateful to have met my new walking partners. It's added a newness to my days. I enjoyed my solitude and have had many meaningful experiences, but sharing a part of this momentous journey with others will create an opportunity for a different kind of growth.

We will reach Lake Geneva in two days' time, near the city of Lausanne. There, Cor will meet his son and his family for a weekend reunion. He will continue his walk after, but it's unlikely I will see him again. I will be walking long days to ensure I reach Rome in time. For now, I'll enjoy the time I have with my new friends.

After Lausanne, Tracy and I continue together—the days idyllic. Much of it is spent walking along wide pathways beside the beautiful Lac Léman, its name in French. In the heat of the afternoons, we find ourselves taking frequent dips in the refreshing water.

Tonight, we will sleep in a Buddhist Monastery high above. A diagonal climb up the steep slope of Mount Pèlerin (French for pilgrim) on a "funicular" (incline railway) leaves us only steps from the monk's door. The views from here are incredible, the lake below and a backdrop of mountains still to be climbed.

The next day, Tracy and I reach Montreux, (passing statues of Charlie Chaplin and Freddie Mercury, both having spent much time here) next to the water, looking out towards snowcapped peaks. Our route then leaves the lake behind and we walk through a valley. We are soon surrounded by mountains on all sides; their heights immense. The most stunning rises slowly and reminds me of a neck atop a set of broad shoulders, sharp-edged and capped in white; it is the aptly named, Mount Blanc. Thankfully, we won't be making that climb. Two nights later we end our day in the mountain town of Martigny in another valley at the base of the Alps. Tomorrow our climb begins.

Tracy's spreadsheet guides us to tonight's accommodation in the cellar of a church Parrish. The space is dimly lit; its barrel ceiling and walls made from stone radiate a damp chill. Inside, a large table, ancient wooden benches, and a handful of metal bunks. Tracy, myself, and four other pilgrims will stay the night. The six of us enjoy a delicious dinner prepared by one of the church's parishioners.

It seems that a good number of people begin their pilgrimage somewhere along the lake. There is a definite feeling of camaraderie with my fellow pilgrims, and I'm happy that English is a language we share. It's not the first language though for the others here tonight; one French, one Swiss, and two Italians, all older than either of us. We talk of our lives back home, but the shared experience of walking each day connects us. After dinner, Tracy and I take a short stroll through the old part of town. The temperature tonight is the coldest yet along my walk. The sun, obviously, has set, but the peaks surrounding us kept it from view.

I've been impressed with how good a hiker Tracy is. I ask, "How did you train for this hike?"

"The gym and walks with my weighted pack," she says. "I'm now in the best shape of my life."

"That's great," I say. "Are you going to keep it up?"

"Without question. I feel great," she says, "When I first started training for my trek, someone told me, 'You're not just working out for a better tomorrow, but a *lifetime* of better tomorrows.' I loved that."

"Me too," I say. I repeat it in my head, working to improve for a lifetime of better tomorrows. This resonates with me. I hadn't thought about my small changes in this way. Over the past year I have been working to improve my body, but more my mind and my spirit, not realizing those improvements will last for a lifetime.

Morning comes and the views get more incredible with every turn of the trail. The valleys are a vibrant green; massive sprinklers turn slowly on the land below. I assume they grow what the many cows we pass along the way will eat. Our route varies, from quiet lanes, ruts in the grass used by the tractors tending to the fields, narrow forest paths, and roads that lead in and out of the many small villages we pass through. In each, we find a fountain with deliciously cold mountain water, and an opportunity to find food.

Another night in a church-sponsored room; no bed tonight, just a mat on the floor. A pilgrim's discount finds Tracy and I dining at the finest restaurant in Orsieres. We need fuel for tomorrow's final climb.

Over dinner, we talk about the upcoming days. Tracy talks of a rest day once we make it down the mountain. I can't afford a day off given my time crunch, and not wanting to skip even a "boring part." We will walk together until the time comes. I enjoy walking with my Aussie friend, and I will miss her. She is down-to-earth, friendly, and accommodating to my wishes. I hope she would say the same.

I turn to Tracy, a hundred meters behind me on the steepest section yet. I stop and take in the scenery. There are patches of snow in the nooks and crannies of the mountain, as well as frequent pops of early spring green, but mostly its gray rocks, the edges look sharp; but when I look ahead, it's a blue sky that dominates my view. I sense the mountain's crest is almost here. When she catches up, we rest for a couple of minutes then start to climb again. This pattern repeats itself for the next hour.

"We must be getting close," I say with barely a grin.

I'm exhausted, but Tracy is really struggling.

"I don't have any energy," she says.

"Have you eaten anything since breakfast?"

"No."

"I think your body just doesn't have enough fuel." I hand her something from my pack.

We stand here, on the side of the mountain, on a super rocky path eating bananas. The view in every direction is stunning.

Next, I take two energy bars from my pack and hand her one. We down those too, and our climb resumes.

Not even twenty minutes later, a building, our home for tonight, comes into view.

"Finally," she says with a forced smile.

We enter the Hospice at the Grand Saint Bernard Pass, passing a sign that shows our elevation – 2573 meters, 8114 feet. This place was founded in the year 962. We check in to the auberge then wander the halls searching for our beds in this massive stone building. The floors are paved with large stone slabs, the walls are plastered white, the light-stained wood on the ceiling is broken up with recessed lights. The interior is more modern than I expect, given its simple exterior. We find out, that indeed, this is the place where the Saint Bernard dog breed was first introduced to the world. In centuries past, these large cold weather dogs have saved thousands of lost skiers and trekkers.

After showers, we take a walk past a small lake next to our home for the night. We are both wearing long pants and puffy jackets, mine a burnt orange Arc'teryx brand, a Christmas gift from my mom. It is cold at this elevation (a thermometer outside says it is seven degrees Celsius/forty-four Fahrenheit) as the sun has already fallen below the mountains to the west. We cross the well-marked border into Italy before scurrying back to the warmth of the hospice.

I look out the window of my dorm room into a dusky light, smiling at where I find myself tonight. I slowly turn my head from side to side, thinking I just climbed the frickin' Alps. It feels good to have done something that I view as major, an accomplishment to remember; something that wasn't even on my radar just a couple weeks ago. I remember a quote that says, a man needs to be ready when an opportunity comes. I'm not sure my climb here is an example of that, but I'm so happy I decided to veer from my original path. Maybe I *should* start to trust myself a little more.

FIFTEEN / descend

July 19 –   Grand Saint Bernard Pass

The view on the way down the mountain is stunning. At our elevation, looking south into Italy, it feels like I'm on top of the world. Clouds are slowly drifting, but the bulk remains blue. The mountains are covered in green with speckles of stone and snow. In the distance, taller mountains line the horizon with even larger patches still covered in white. I walk, slack jawed, for much of the day.

Together we follow narrow paths cut through green pastures; our descent much gentler than our climb. On our way up the mountain, we didn't see many other hikers but today we see several pairs ahead and behind. While devouring our communal meals back at the hospice, we met many fellow travelers. Most, here to hike the surrounding mountains; the hospice, their base camp. We also met an Italian couple headed in the opposite direction of ours, headed to Santiago in Spain. A handful, like us, are walking to Rome.

Over the next several days, we slowly descend from the crest, often next to ancient stone aqueducts carrying melted snow further down the mountain to irrigate the crops in the narrow valleys below. Sleeping in the towns of Gignod, Nus, and then Borgo, where we dine with a family in their home which sits below a castle abandoned a century ago.

In Ivrea, a proper city, our expected lodgings are unavailable. A canoe club here has bunks for pilgrims on the Via Francigena but not tonight, as they are hosting a race. Shortly after learning of this, the rain starts to fall. We walk in our rain gear to one hotel and are told "completo". At the next place, we get the same response. It turns out the canoe race is actually a whitewater world championship. We start to notice signs posted all over the city. Everything is booked.

Tracy says, "I want to stop at the Decathlon," a large sporting goods store. "I need a net for my head. The mosquitos are supposed to be bad by the rice fields we will be walking through for days."

"Great idea," I say.

We splash our way in a what has become a downpour, my shoes squishing with each step. Our walk is long, our destination being on the outskirts on the far side of town. This is the worst weather I've experienced so far on my walk, but Tracy and I laugh our way through the town's center.

Our walk is all for naught. They don't have anything that will help protect our faces, but we buy a few things anyway. I find a long sleeve button-up shirt to replace the one I left hanging on a branch to dry a week ago. I'll need it cover my arms as we walk through what I now imagine to be swarms of the pesky insects.

Tracy and I are both on our phones inside the front of the store, calling ahead to find beds for tonight. So far, we've struck out.

"Can I help you find something?" a pretty middle-aged woman asks, a Decathlon shopping bag in hand. "Or do you need a ride?" Her English is perfect.

A tall twenty-something man stands at her side.

"No, that's okay," I say. "We're calling to find a place to stay."

"We are walking the Via Francigena," Tracy says. "Our expected accommodation, the canoe club, is not available."

"Yes, the race," she says.

A couple of seconds later, she says, "You'll come with us. We will not let you sleep in the rain."

We do.

"We don't live far, and we have a spare room," she says, as she drives her minivan out of the parking lot. "This is my son, Alberto. I am Lara. My husband, Enrico, will be home later. Pietro, my other son is home now."

We tell her a little about our walk as she drives along narrow roads. She soon turns onto a lane with maybe ten large homes. She pulls into the drive of a modernly designed house and enters a two-car garage. She leads us inside and we set our packs, rain covers still dripping, and soaked shoes, just inside the door.

We are introduced to Pietro. The five of us sit around a large banquette in the kitchen talking, and Lara hands us towels. She offers us tea and we happily accept. Pietro, his accent obvious, says he has always wanted to "take this walk," and says, someday he will. He works in Germany but is home on holiday. Alberto, a student at university, is on break.

"It is rare for them both to be home at the same time."

A half an hour later, freshly showered and changed, we are back in the kitchen, talking while Lara prepares dinner. Our wet clothes, and any dirty clothes we had, are now being washed and dried, having been collected by our hosts.

Enrico walks in with a large smile, a text alerting him to his unexpected guests.

Over dinner we learn that Enrico is an architect and designed their beautiful home. We enjoy an after-dinner expresso and later a glass of wine on a second story patio. Together we watch the sky change from orange to purple to black.

I lay on an air mattress, delivered by Enrico and say "Goodnight" to Tracy laying in the bed. I smile at our luck today and am grateful for the generosity we've received.

***

The dreaded mosquitos are nowhere to be found. The intense summer heat must have something to do with it. The yards of mesh we found in a small village shop selling hardware, toasters, and everything in-between, remain tucked in our packs.

For days we walk through the fields where tomorrow's risotto grows. Our walk takes us closer to the Po River, the namesake for the broad valley in which we now trek. Our days remain long; rising with the sun, walking, only stopping to eat, or when we find an infrequent opportunity for shade.

Reaching the tiny village of Corte Sant'Andrea, we check into the pilgrim-only ostello; a donation is all that is asked. Another stamp is added in my pilgrim's passport which is now becoming a visual representation of my walk along the Via. Tonight's home is one of only a handful of buildings in this ancient town and it is attached to the village church.

Several familiar faces are here tonight, having seen them over the last few nights in our other pilgrim's accommodations. Six of us head to dinner at the only place we find offering food. We enter through a beaded curtain instead of a door. These hanging beads have become common. I've learned it's to keep the flies out, while still letting the fresh air in—smart. It feels like we have stepped back in time; a feeling I've grown accustomed to on this walk. I imagine not much has changed in this place over the last fifty years. Renato, our host, is charming, though I don't understand a word. Typical pilgrim conversation of our lives back home and stories of our walk thus far make for a lively dinner. My meal, ravioli and risotto, is delicious. We don't languish over dinner like most nights, as others are waiting to be seated. We order two bottles of wine, taking them to go. The six of us walk to the river we will be crossing in the morning and watch as the sun falls below the horizon.

The river crossing is said to be a memorable one. Tracy said she's read about it on several blogs. At 7:00 am the next morning, twelve pilgrims, two with bikes, board a smallish flat-bottom fishing boat with a large motor attached.

Danilo is our captain, an older man with thinning gray hair and a joyous smile. He has been ferrying pilgrims across this river for over forty years. For a small fee, we get transport across the river to his home, a ten-minute ride down the Po. He gives a short talk about the history of this section of our walk, the Italian pilgrims translate as needed. He offers juice and snacks, then opens a large book, the binding at least five inches thick. One by one, we take a seat next to him. He stamps our passport with an ornate and extra-large stamp as we enter our name into his ancient register, filled with the names of all those who have come before. After the last pilgrim enters their name, he hugs each of us, and kisses each cheek. It is a moving experience.

On our walk towards Piacenza the next day, Tracy tells me, "I am going to be taking a rest day tomorrow. According to my calculations, I still have an extra seven days."

That means *I* still need to make up about three days.

"I have to keep going," I say.

"I know, Jack. You have some long days ahead," she says. "I plan on slowing down with the climbs up ahead."

The route heads into the Apennine Mountains in a few days, and I must push myself to make it on time. I will not be walking sixteen-hour days like the first part of my walk, but I plan on some longer ones.

Tonight, Tracy and I have dinner at the fanciest place we have dined so far, and she insists on picking up the tab. She has booked a room in a nice hotel for tomorrow, but tonight she is staying at the pilgrim's place. After we brush our teeth but before we head to our bunks, we say our farewell, uncertain if she'll be awake when I head out in the morning.

"You have helped me so much," I say. "It was amazing to get to know you. I hope we keep in touch. I'll be sure to let you know of any interesting places I stay."

"It was my pleasure," she says with a big smile. "I so enjoyed our time together. If Cor catches up to me, I'll let you know."

We share a long embrace.

In bed, I think again of my good fortune. Meeting Tracy and Cor changed my walk for the better. Meeting those on this pilgrimage would not have happened had I followed my original route. My walk would have remained a solitary journey. The people along the way have added much to my adventure. After the last few weeks of starting each day with friends, I will start out alone again tomorrow.

***

The next few days have some hard climbs. I enjoy meals with fellow pilgrims most every night. The number of others walking the Via has steadily increased in the last week or so; the pilgrims range from others my age to those in their sixties. English is spoken by most, but not all I meet. Most mornings I start out with a pilgrim or two, but normally, with our paces varied, I pull ahead. Making up time is still at the front of my mind. Each night there are new faces along with a couple familiar ones. The options in the mountains are limited. Happily, I have made up one day already, having walked one extra-long day, over forty kilometers, and I spent last night in the woods.

I enter the town of Pontremoli, which sits in a valley surrounded by mountains, still solo. It's beautiful and is the first decent size city since Piacenza. Despite the fact it's not yet 3:00 pm, I stop for the day. My legs, and more importantly my feet, could use a break. After finding food, I search for a place to do laundry. My clothes and I both stink.

I find a laundromat in the town center. I change into my rain gear in a small bathroom and go commando. It takes a few minutes, and Google Translate, to figure out how to start the machine. I empty my pack of every piece of clothing, and throw it all in. Detergent is added automatically—sweet.

I sit in a chair, waiting. After hearing mostly Italian the last two days, my ears perk up when I hear a middle-aged couple speaking English.

"Hello," I say when I make eye contact with the woman.

"Hi," she says. "Are you walking the Via Francigena?"

"Yes," I say excitedly. "Are you?"

She laughs, then says, "No, we are on holiday. We have a place here, but we live in the U.S."

"Me too. I live in Wisconsin. Where are you from?"

"Michigan, we're neighbors," she says. "Mario's family is from here. We bought an apartment in town a few years ago and had it restored. We now come here every summer."

"Wow, how cool."

Mario chimes in. "I used to come here as a kid and loved it. Once I retired, we found our place here." Retired? He looks too young to be retired.

"I'm Jack." I reach out my hand.

"Nice to meet you. I haven't met many Americans here," he says. "This is my wife, Anne."

They quiz me about my trip so far, and we talk briefly about our lives back home.

Their laundry is done long before mine. Once they have everything folded and are ready to go, Mario asks, "Would you like to have drinks later? There is a nice bar on the square near our place."

"I'd love to."

Once I change back into clean clothes, and the rest are rolled up and put back into ultralight packing cubes, I head to my hoped-for accommodations. I enter another castle on a hill, this one overlooks the city. Gold and Maroon flags wave with the breeze. "Yes, there are beds available in the dorm," I am told by a woman behind the desk, her accent making her words sound poetic.

"Fantastico," I say.

"The castle will close at nine, but I will give you a key for the gate, so you can exit in the morning," she says. "Just place the key into the box once you re-lock the gate."

I walk along the castle's walls. One side looks down into small courtyards, the other looks out toward the mountains and the city. I find my dorm room, filled with ten empty bunks. I shower, put my clothes back on, and then wander through my eerily empty home for tonight. I see not a soul.

I meet Mario on the patio of the bar. He takes my order and then goes to get the drinks.

"Anne will join us later," he says.

I tell him about my difficulties as a student. He tells me how he occupies his days since retirement. He is fifty-eight, retired early, tired of a life "punching a clock." He talks excitedly about the renovation of their place here, and how they enjoy their summer travels across Europe.

Anne joins us for a final drink, and they invite me to dinner at a local restaurant. Afterwards, we walk to their apartment along narrow alleyways which get narrower as we go. It's surreal how narrow the passages are. With my arms stretched, I can just about reach the houses on each side. I love it. Not two minutes from the restaurant, we enter a door and climb a flight of stairs. The apartment is lovely; crisp white walls, a small but modern kitchen, a small dining table, a sofa, and two chairs fill the small space. A few pieces of modern art are scattered on two walls, and a dozen framed photos create a collage on another.

"Anne loves taking pictures," Mario says.

"They're beautiful," I say, looking at her. They are.

"Gelato?" Anne asks.

"Si."

We talk over scoops of Pistachio before I say goodnight to these new, unexpected friends.

I walk back through the maze of passageways and up to my castle. The gate is already locked. I use my extra-large key to enter, then lock myself in. I climb the ancient stone steps leading to my room. Looking down, I spot a young family of three playing under a hazy light in the courtyard below. The scene warms my heart. I grab my puffy coat, as the temperature has dropped, and wander the walkways along the outside walls and look up to a star-filled sky. My mouth opens wider and my head shakes in amazement at simply being here … now.

SIXTEEN / pilgrim

August 2 – Marinella di Sarzana, Italy

I wade into warm water, my pack resting on my travel towel on a sandy beach; my "farmers" tan in all its glory. I swim out twenty meters and turn to see green hills rising from the water to the north, then dozens of umbrellas in every possible color planted in the sand in front of me. I have made it to my original target—the Mediterranean Sea.

I swim out as fast as I can and as far as I dare, then float on my back. I look up to a pure blue sky. Birds pass overhead, looking down. It feels amazing. I'm completely relaxed, the salty waters restoring my body which I've pushed hard over the last two months.

I still can't believe I'm here, where every day brings something new. It's so different from my days the past year, when I was in a routine—reading, writing, and walking each day. There were a few adventures—skiing, hiking, sailing, but for the most part, I was inside my bubble, content. Content that I was making progress towards something yet unknown.

This walk, too, has its routine; walking, fueling my body, and finding an inexpensive place to rest. And like my life over the last year, lots of time to think. What is different on this journey, though, is I have gotten to know others from different cultures around the globe. My mind has been opened, and new friends have been made. I think of Nathalie, her smile, her touch; our time together, a reminder that life is meant to be shared. It's both the people part, *and* the solitude of this adventure that has helped me grow.

The last week has been another solitary section, outwalking nearly everyone I meet. But my evenings in the ostellos have brought the camaraderie I now seek. Now, I am eager to walk with others again. My time crunch had me pushing hard to get on pace to reach Rome. Those efforts have paid off. I'm happy I can finally slow my gait and embrace the opportunity to develop deeper connections with those I am bound to meet.

This afternoon, I pass through Carrara where the marble for Davinci's David was born. The mountains here have sides of white, the quarries still busy. Roads of marble switchbacks, zig-zagging up and over the heights. It is quite the sight. I march on, reaching the town of Pietrasanta, and score one of five beds reserved for pilgrims in a convent overlooking the town square. The city is lovely, and I dine with pilgrims I'd yet to encounter.

The next morning, my pace relaxed, I walk with four others I dined with last night. I am stopping in six hours when we reach Lucca. I've read it is a Tuscan highlight. Stopping here is a must, the city built centuries ago, is encircled by an ancient wall. We reach the town in the early afternoon and find our beds, reserved while on our way. After our post-walk rituals, yes, a nap too, we walk together; our cadre has grown. We are two Italians, a Dutch, a French, another Aussie, a Swiss father and son, and me. We ramble en masse, no destination. We stop for drinks at a bar on a small town square. I feel a little buzzed after failing to honor my two-drink rule.

We listen to a suggestion and make a reservation for dinner. At the appointed time, we are seated in the round. After the waiter brings our drinks, I surprise myself, and stand.

"I want to say how great it's been to get to know each of you, even if it has been only for a short time. This is my first walk, and it's much more than I expected. I know some of you only started recently, and others have been taking these walks for years, but for me, the journey has been magical."

I raise my glass and say "Cin Cin."

I sit, look down and grin. I am proud of myself for making the toast. I can't imagine having done that, even with a group of my college friends. Speeches in high school and college always had me on edge. I can't think of anything I feared more. I hope tonight was a turning point in my ability to speak clearly, expressing my true feelings, sincerely. In this moment, I think of my dad and ask if he's proud.

I spend much of the meal talking to Bruno, the father, and oldest of our crew. He talks of the recent change in his mindset, valuing time above all else. Though from what I gather, money is not a concern.

"I used to identify so closely with my job, it was my purpose, and my focus. When I retired, I lost all that," Bruno explains. "I did not know who I was. That is why I took this walk, to help figure it out."

"I hadn't thought about losing your identity when you retire," I say. An instant later, I think of Lily. I hadn't known her when she made her transition, but she must have gone through something similar, or maybe she still is.

As we leave the restaurant, I ask, "Does anyone want to walk the wall surrounding the city?" I decided last night to make this walk after reading an article online about Lucca.

"It's getting late," someone says.

"How long is it?" Bruno asks.

"Just over four K," I respond.

"Too long for me," I hear someone else say.

"I think I'll pass," Bruno says. "And don't forget about the curfew." The ostello closes its doors at eleven.

"No worries. I'll see you all in the morning," I say as I turn to find the stairs leading up.

I walk along the wall, its width about a hundred feet wide, the tree-lined pedestrian path, well-lit. I find dozens of others atop the wall, many walking hand in hand, others pedal bicycles slowly, or in one case, a youngster on his trike. My gaze is varied, looking down into this enchanting city, or watching those pass by, or like now, up to the sky.

This walking life has led me here, and to the happiest I can remember being. I ask the question, "Why?" My answer, after some thought, "Simplicity. A quieted mind. The people. And a sense of adventure." Walking under the stars in a new place each night has become one of my new favorite things.

We're up early, and together, we walk. I didn't mention, but I'm in Tuscany now and have been since my swim in the sea. It starts to feel like I imagined, rolling hills and cypress trees reaching for the sky. The hill towns come—San Miniato, San Gimignano, Monteriggioni—and go. I walk opened-mouthed for much of the day, the landscape is that stunning. As I walk from one hill town to the next, it often feels like I'm walking through a painting, all under the fabulous Tuscan sun. I take some amazing photos. The colors of the landscape, ever-changing, are more vibrant than I've seen before. I'm told it's the light, but I am unsure why it seems so special.

This afternoon we reach Sienna, and from what I've read is one of the most beautiful cities in all of Tuscany. If the crowds are any judge, I'm tempted to agree. Me and five of our current band of pilgrims are sharing an Airbnb tonight, as all the pilgrim's accommodations were full. After a shower, I leave my friends and head out to explore.

I walk through narrow streets bustling with people. I have no particular destination, but soon find myself in the center of Piazza del Campo, a massive town square, though its shape is that of a scallop shell. It is surrounded by stands constructed for the upcoming Palio, a horse race where ten horses will circle the medieval town square, each representing one of the city's "contrades" or city wards. The outside part of the piazza is already covered in clay, the color of the burnt sienna crayon in my last box of sixty-four.

I reserve a time to climb the Torre del Mangia, the tower located on the square. I sit in the center of the piazza to people-watch and wait. When my time comes, I start to climb. I get winded halfway up the four hundred or so steps to the top of the tower. It's a good thing I'm not claustrophobic, it's a tight squeeze in places, and other tourists are just inches ahead and behind. When I reach the top, I'm amazed by the views. I walk around the tower's crown, looking in each direction. The green hills of the countryside go on for miles, all under a cerulean sky, with small patches of clouds scattered about. Every building and roof are the same burnt sienna, most faded by the centuries. The only exception, the massive Duomo, with its stunning black and white stripes.

After my descent, I continue to wander through the busy streets alone. Looking for quiet, I move away from the city center. As always, thoughts come, and soon float away. Occasionally, I think of Nathalie, though she no longer sticks in my mind.

I find a bench and sit to watch an old man with his craft. A metal worker, pounding a glowing orange piece of steel. An hour passes, his skills impress. His passion for his art is obvious.

Leaving Sienna, two hundred kilometers remain. I fly out a week from tomorrow, my return ticket booked while in Lausanne for the last possible day. My walking companions remain pretty much the same. We stay in church-sponsored accommodations, often convents, as we make our way. The days pass quickly, and the evenings of conversation are enlightening; I'm surprised by how similar our views on life.

Over the past weeks, I've noticed a change in myself. I'm becoming more comfortable in my own skin. I am now the first to approach someone new, my head up, a smile, and a nod. I've realized with a smile, a simple question, and sincere listening, most people will open up and share of themselves. These are the moments I cherish most.

My arrival at St. Peters Square in the late afternoon is cause for celebration. Many photos are taken, and hugs are shared. My latest crew and I go for drinks; we toast to "new friends," but soon we must part, each person's Roman accommodation is scattered about.

As I walk from Vatican City, reality sinks in—my walking life is over; I fly home tomorrow. I feel a sense of accomplishment, of course, but my arrival is not what I expected. It's too abrupt an end. If I could continue walking, I would; the where doesn't matter; to keep moving with others, that's the thing. I don't want this journey to end.

For months I have pushed away thoughts of what life has in store for me when I return home. I've done well focusing on the "now." Tonight, as I walk along busy streets, horns honking, people shouting, my mind races.

SEVENTEEN / write

September 18 —   Madison, Wisconsin

I get out of my Uber and head toward the front door, my well-worn pack in tow. Lily is in the doorway, smiling—we embrace. For some reason, I've been nervous about *this* reunion. We head to the kitchen and take our favorite seats. Within minutes, my stomach and mind relax as we fall into our comfortable routine … talking, sharing. I tell her my plan.

Fast forward three weeks.

I walk across a large and airy space and find my favorite seat in the heart of the hushed room and set up for the next four hours. My phone is set to "do not disturb."

I lift the screen on my MacBook Air, and open my current project in the Scrivener App. Then I scroll through the photos from my trip; I think of the day, and where I was emotionally when each image was snapped. With each photo, I think of a story I can tell. When something resonates, I write. This pattern has continued every day since my return.

I'm not sure what my end product will be, but a book is what's in my mind. On my flight home, I thought about how the walk changed me. Now, the idea of sharing my journey with others has become my focus.

A little after 11:00 am, I pack up and walk out of the Law Library, it's my favorite on campus; I like its open feel. I head back to Lily's, thinking of my life before coming here; lost and unsure of who I was. It reminds me of how far I've come.

The first few days after my return were an adjustment, as I worked my way into a new routine. Now writing is my passion; it elevates my life. I'm grateful for having found my latest thing to be enthusiastic about.

As I walk, Stephen King's voice plays in my ears, his book, *On Writing*, is my latest how-to. I've already finished Anne Lamont's *Bird by Bird* and a book written a century ago, E.M Forster's, *Aspects of the Novel*. I'm learning how to write—getting advice on how to convey what I intend. Each day I'm excited to get to my seat, my writing is constantly at the front of my mind. Like on my walk, where the goal was reaching Rome, now finishing my book is the far-off dream. But as I learned, it's the journey that excites me—to progress in my writing—that's the meaningful thing.

My habit of reading is back, after a break during the last half of my walk. Reading the first part of Cal Newport's book, *Deep Work*, has helped form my new routine.

As always, I take the long way back home. Today is a beautiful day—the is sun shining, and there is a gentle breeze. My daily walks are a reminder of my recent life on the move.

"There's a salad in the fridge if you're hungry," Lily says. Carole King's voice plays quietly in the background.

"Thanks, I am. Are you?"

"Yes. I was just waiting on you."

I take the salad out and grab two oversized bowls. We sit at the island and eat our lunch.

"How did it go today?" She asks.

"Great. I think I've only got a week or so left of writing my scenes. Then I can start weaving in the lessons."

"Do you remember last year, early on, when I asked about your core values?"

"And I said, I have no idea," I laugh.

"Have you thought about that in all your self-reflection?"

"Of course. I have worked to identify the kind of person I want to be."

"Good. Be sure to include that in your book too."

Later in the week, I head to a deli downtown. Steven, Lily's friend and advisor, said he had something to discuss. I take a seat and look out onto the street. When Steven arrives, we each order the Cuban.

I tell him about my adventure, and what I've been doing since my return. He shares stories of his family's trip to the Pacific Northwest.

"Wow, it sounds amazing," I say. "I can't wait to make it there someday."

"So, on to why I asked you to meet."

"I was wondering."

"Are you interested in a job?"

"Doing what?" I inquire.

"Project management," he says. "I have a client that is looking for some help running his businesses. He has three, and he's spread himself too thin. He asked me if I knew of someone he could trust."

"Really?" I say, surprised by the offer.

"It would be *pretty* good money," he says with raised brows. "I was surprised at how good."

"Wow. I appreciate you thinking of me," I say. A second later I add, "But, I'm not sure."

"You get along with people. People like you," he says. "That's what this guy is looking for."

This wasn't on my radar. At first, it sounds too good to be true. "Let me think about it while we eat."

"Of course, there's no rush. Take a few days." A few seconds later he asks, "So, how is your book coming along?"

"Good," I respond excitedly, "I love the process."

Soon our waitress delivers our sandwiches and two glasses of water. While we eat, Steven tells me, "Lauren is changing majors again. At this rate, she'll be in school for years."

"I'm really not one to speak, with my history, but I think it's good she's trying to find something she enjoys now, while she's still in school."

"I understand that, but she needs to pick something, graduate, and start a career."

"That's your generation," I respond after swallowing a big bite. "Give her some time. I'm sure her classes are mostly gen ed up to this point anyway."

He nods and takes a bite.

I continue to turn over the idea of working a full-time job. The idea of making good money without going back to school is appealing, and being secure financially has always been my focus. Then I think about the time commitment, and how much I enjoy my morning writing, and the plans I'm already forming for my next trip.

Before I finish my sandwich, I say, "I appreciate you thinking of me, but I don't think I'm interested in pursuing a full-time job right now. I'm loving my writing and thinking about what I really want to do with my life. Plus, I don't want to give up travel. I need to find something that allows me a lot of time off."

"Okay, I understand," he says with a scrunched-up face. Surprised.

After lunch, I put in my Air Pods and head to meet up with Jimmy. As I cross the campus on this beautiful fall day, I listen to the album, *The Calm Within,* by my new favorite artist, Rob Riccardo. Normally, my days aren't busy, just the library, a walk with the dogs, then home. I also volunteer at the Senior Center two days a week.

I'm excited to see Jimmy; our first meeting since my trip. I walk past a Starbucks; the line of cars runs into the street. I shake my head, thinking the world's gone insane; the time and money people spend for a cup of caffeine. A minute later, relief, as I see a "Practice Kindness" bumper sticker. I smile.

I remove my earbuds and step down into a basement bar.

"Hey, Jack," Jimmy says when he sees me.

"Hey," I say with a huge smile.

"It's great to see you. My mom told me about your trip."

"Yeah, it was amazing. I'm so glad I went."

"I can't wait to hear about it."

"Yeah, for sure," I say. "So, how is your mom?"

"Holding steady." I can tell he's surprised that I've asked about someone else.

"Good," I say, catching his eye.

I enjoy hanging out with Jimmy, and I sense that he does too. As always, he's focused on getting good grades; and he talks about grad school. Going out like this is good for him, I think. I have two drinks, honoring my self-imposed limit.

On my way home it starts to sprinkle. This is unexpected. I try to stay dry walking next to buildings, dashing from one to the next, but soon the sky opens, and it starts to pour. I accept my fate—walking arms open, looking up, and laughing—living in the moment.

I enter the kitchen, sopping wet, welcomed by the soundtrack from *Les Mis*. "Something smells good." I say to Lily, who is standing at the sink. Then, "Sorry," as I dart to my room, dripping all the way.

A few minutes later I'm back, sitting at the island, watching her julienne a zucchini. I feel a bit guilty that I am home later than I expected. Since my return, I've been helping her with dinner. I'm now her full-time sous chef.

"I'm not going to the lecture in *this*," she says, looking out the window. She winks.

"Fine by me," I say, "I'll just write."

"I'll call and let Ben know we aren't going," she says, adding, "Firecracker Salmon is on the menu tonight."

"Yay!" She knows it's my favorite.

"Would you like to join me for a glass of wine? I've opened one of your bottles, the Chianti." The assortment was my gift to Lily, from some of the regions I'd walked through.

"Absolutely."

"I was speaking to Steven earlier," she says, "and he mentioned you had a possible job offer, but you weren't interested."

They must talk more often than I realize.

"Yeah. It sounded like a decent job, though I wasn't sure of the details. But in the long run, I knew it wasn't for me. I don't want a job just because it pays well."

"I'm glad you realize that now."

I flash a close-mouthed smile.

"I want to finish my writing project first. That's my focus now."

She puts her hand on my forearm. She looks at me and says, "Right answer, Jack."

I feel relief at her response. I was worried she would think me lazy, or selfish, for not accepting an offer so generous.

"Plus, I want to travel again."

"Have you thought about becoming a travel writer?"

"Actually, it has crossed my mind, but I don't want to just write about travel and different places."

"Travel writing is not always just about places. It's about the story—and how each adventure changes you."

"That I like!"

A thought comes into my head but I hesitate to speak it out loud. Over the past year I've spent a lot of time thinking, reading, and meeting new people. I've come to the realization … I *can* live a life more daring than most. A life I didn't imagine before.

"I don't want to sound cocky," I tell her, "But, I am starting to realize the person I can become. I want to focus on that for now. I think that is why I passed on Steven's offer. I want something—bigger." I shrug.

"Do you have a far-reaching goal in mind?"

"Far-reaching…" I repeat, trying to think of a good response. A few seconds later I say, "Positively impacting people—maybe with my writing."

"Another good answer." She smiles.

"I've been thinking a lot while working on my book. I'm so glad I read so much before my walk. I think the books maybe opened my mind, then travel, the seeds of experience, allowed me to have some interesting insights," I say. "Like, I didn't think everyone would be so similar. I thought living in a different country would make people think differently than me, but I found we all pretty much strive for the same things."

"I hadn't thought of it in those terms," she says. "I like it."

I remain silent, thinking how to use this idea in my book.

"Your life is a blank canvas, Jack." Lily says with a broad smile, "What will you create?"

***

While writing has become my passion, I still enjoy other things. I play the guitar most evenings and working in the garden is no longer just a chore. The Hoofers outings with Mary always bring me joy. Time passes and my word count grows.

One fall weekend, my family visits, meeting Lily for the first time. As my mom witnesses my life here, I see a smile in her eyes. No longer worried about me, my life seemingly on track.

Over dinner on their first night, one I helped create, my mom and Lily talk about their lives; both laughing, a sound that warms my heart.

My brothers seem as happy to see me, as I am them. They join me on a walk through town, as my canine friends lead the way. Sunday night, we all share another meal. We laugh and talk about a family vacation over Spring Break.

My book is slowly taking shape. I've edited all the ramblings I entered while on my walk; sifting through for any nuggets, organizing by theme. I flip through my index file, looking for fitting quotes. This project has become like a puzzle, though not as easy as a toddler's wooden ten piece. I outline the book—from my days being lost, to my arrival in Rome, and to my return home. I think this book can be good, but finishing it, seems a long, long way off.

As with my past writing efforts, Lily and Mary are my first readers, each giving their critique. One day, Mary asks, "Can I share this with my friend? She's an editor here in town."

A week later, I meet her friend, Sophie, for coffee.

She is younger than I expected, attractive, with short brown hair. I'd guess she's in her late thirties. She wears a pair of modern glasses, both oversized and green.

"It's nice to finally meet you. I've heard so many stories."

"Same here," I say. "Mary mentioned she sent you something last year."

"Yes, and when she told me you were writing about your adventure, I couldn't wait to read it. I've read the first five chapters. I think you've got something here, and I like it in first person."

"That's good to hear. First person is the easiest for me. Plus, I've gotten some good pointers from both Mary and Lily."

We talk about my trip and my writing routine. She tells me of her travels, mostly in her "younger days," and about life with a six-year-old.

After I finish my second coffee, we agree to meet again in about a month, after Thanksgiving. "Email your completed chapters as you finish them," she says. "Would you mind if I put on my editor's hat as I review your work?"

"That would be great."

"I'll bring whatever I have received to our next meeting."

Outside, we say our goodbyes, and share a quick hug.

On the one point three mile walk back to Lily's, I think the meeting went well, but begin to worry if I can come up with enough to complete a sixty-to-seventy-thousand-word book. Like the flip of a switch, my stomach starts to churn and my forehead starts to sweat. I think, this project just got real.

Since returning in September, the scale of my "exchange" with Lily has remained out of balance. I've offered to do more and carry my weight, but Lily insists my presence is welcome, regardless of the scale. Always, I do what she asks, and look for any need. We live happily, following our own routines.

If writing had become my passion, now it's also my full-time job. My library time extends well into the afternoon. Then I walk, despite any cold, and head straight to my room.

By Christmas, my first draft is done. Sophie has edited most of the book, giving me rewriting assignments, and deadlines. Use the five senses, cut this, and add that. I rewrite sections, and soon begin to polish.

The sense of accomplishment I feel when I read my nearly completed work is overwhelming.

I send the final chapters to Sophie. We are to meet next week.

> *Human beings, it seems, are at their best when immersed deeply in something challenging.*
>
> Cal Newport, *Deep Work: Rules for Focused Success in a Distracted World*

> *Your job isn't to find these ideas but to recognize them when they show up."*
>
> Stephen King, *On Writing: A Memoir of the Craft*

EIGHTEEN / celebrate

April 30 –   Madison, Wisconsin

It's now months later as Lily, Ben, Mary, and I walk along a broad sidewalk, making our way through the crowd. Downtown is busy on this lively Friday night. State Street is glistening, the temperature warmer than I would expect for an early Spring evening. It rained most of the day, but the sky is now clear, and the sun is about to set. I walk next to Mary. Both she and Lily are in dresses, and Ben's in a suit. I'm wearing a steel blue button-down shirt, a sport coat, a deeper shade of blue, and a pair of khakis, all bought for the occasion. In such semi-formal attire, I felt awkward at first, but after a two-mile walk it feels okay and proper for why we are here.

We head towards the Capitol, veering off when we reach its perimeter. Dinner tonight is at a fancy restaurant, L'Etoile, French for "The Star." We find Steven and his family standing at the bar, chatting with Sophie. Everyone is dressed to impress.

We are soon seated; I'm between Lily and Steven, and directly across from Lauren.

"Congratulations," Lauren says, reaching out to touch my hand.

"Thanks. It is kind of cool. I think I may have found my thing." I smile at her and shrug.

She smiles back, "So lucky. I'm still searching for mine, but I think I'm close."

I've met Lauren several times since moving to Madison. She's more beautiful than cute, long dark hair, and a slender face. At first glance, I'd assume she's probably a snob, looking like the college girls who acted like they were too good for me. However, knowing her, I'd be wrong—but she is out of my league.

"So, how are your …," I hesitate, "history classes, I think?"

"Nope. I've changed yet again," she says with a smirk. "This time in a totally different direction, Landscape Architecture. It's my favorite yet. I want to design *and* work with my hands."

"That's great," I say with a big smile. It sounds interesting to me. "I, too, have begun to really enjoy that—getting my hands dirty, working in the garden and tinkering around Lily's house."

The waitress arrives at our table and takes our drink orders. Ben also orders appetizers for the table. When the waitress leaves, Lauren says, "It's going to take me an extra year. My parents aren't thrilled about that."

"It's much better to find something you enjoy now," I say. "I didn't find anything that excited me in my first two years of school."

"I have to admit, I haven't read your book yet," she says sheepishly. "My dad told me, a couple of times that I should."

I laugh and say, "That's okay. I know most our age don't read unless it's for a class. But I think you'll like it; I know you like to travel."

"Yes, I fell in love with it," she says. "So, what's it about?"

"The gist of the book is why you should travel, *and* the benefits of solitude. I talk about how travel made me look at myself and question who I was. I found I am stronger and more courageous than I thought. I share what I learned on my walk and what *I* think is important in life."

"*The Journey Never Ends* … How did you come up with that title?"

"Well, the book follows me on my walk last year. It's a take on the whole, 'it's the journey, not the destination' idea. In the book, I share about how I went on the walk for the adventure, but it was so much more. Then I return home, and my life's journey continues."

Lauren glances at her dad, sees him talking to her mom, and quietly says, "I hope to travel again this summer, but I haven't discussed it with my parents yet. I want to experience New Zealand."

"That's great. I want to get there someday," I say. "I'm headed back to Europe for another walk."

"What country?"

"Starting in Munich and walking to Spain. I'll be in four different countries. It's another pilgrimage, so there should be cheap places to stay. That's a must for me. Plus, you meet lots of people from around the world by staying in the hostel kind of places."

"It sounds fun, but walking a thousand miles—I don't know."

"It *is* fun," I say excitedly. "The walking grows on you. By the end, you won't want to stop."

"Maybe someday," she says. "Back to what you find important. What did you learn?"

"That I need certain things to be happy. Mainly, something to be enthusiastic about, finding connections, valuing my time more, and that you don't need a whole lot to be happy."

"And you learned that by walking?"

"Well, really the solitude. I was alone for weeks, with little human interaction. I had lots of time to think. I also talk about travel in general. I think it's so valuable to travel *and* find solitude when you're young."

I ask Lauren, "Were you solo on your travels?"

"Most of the time, but a friend came for a bit."

"Traveling by yourself forces so much growth," I say "Did you feel different when you got back home?

"I did. Like I don't stress about things as much anymore, knowing things will work out. I had a few mishaps on my trip, but I got everything figured out."

"I know," I say. "You only have yourself. It feels great knowing you can solve your own problems."

We share stories about our travels.

"I couldn't believe the kindness I experienced," she says.

"I know. Before my walk, I had started to think there was a shortage of kindness, but travel taught me that the more you put yourself out there, the more goodness you'll see."

"I made some good friends while I was away," she says.

"Yeah, me too. I love the people you meet when traveling," I say. "I've found you usually share similar interests, and it's amazing how the conversations can get deep right away. I walked with an Italian guy my age for a while, and we talked about our dreams, childhoods, and struggles to find our path in life within the first hour of meeting."

'I know," she says, her eyes widening. "That's why I want to keep traveling."

"Me too. I've made some amazing connections. That is so rare in our day-to-day lives."

"Maybe we can meet up on campus—after I read your book."

"Sure thing. I'd love to."

I wonder what she thinks of me. I bet she's impressed that I wrote a book, though not enough to have read it. Maybe our shared love of travel is intriguing to her. I'm happy she wants to meet up … maybe she is attracted to me.

Our waitress brings out the drinks. When everyone has theirs in hand, Lily stands. "I want to congratulate Jack on having his first book published. He's put his heart and soul into it. I've seen him continue his work, trying to make a difference in the lives of those he meets."

My eyes well up.

Lily raises her glass. "To Jack."

Everyone else raises theirs. "To Jack."

I can feel myself blush at the attention. I'm proud to have completed it and excited to have people read it. A part of me likes the attention, but, I would prefer to stay out of the limelight.

"I can't wait to read your *next* book," Mary says.

"I'm not sure I have material for another book. Though who knows after my next trip."

Emily taps my shoulder as she leans behind Steven, and says, "What are you doing this summer?"

"I'm walking the Camino de Santiago—starting in Germany. I'll have to take a train part of the way, but I plan to walk the entirety of Spain."

"I've always wanted to do that. It's been on my bucket list since college," she says. "I can't imagine the beauty you'll see. Well, also, what you've already seen. I really liked your book; that walk sounded fantastic."

"Yes, it was. I've been very lucky."

"I'm glad you realize that."

"Trust me, I do," I say, as our eyes lock.

She gives me a smile and nods.

"I'm addicted to walking long distances," I say. "I'm also headed to Finland for a week this time, then I'll fly to Munich."

"Yes, Steven said you were going to visit Johannes and Emilia. You'll love it there. We stayed with them a few years back."

"Lily insisted I go. She's excited for me to meet them."

"So, Jack," Ben says, "I know, *you* know, that we've all been a good influence on you. Your gratitude is always on display. But let me say what an influence you've been to this old crew."

"If me hanging around is good for you—great! And I really do appreciate all your support. Trust me, this book would not have happened without all your help."

I look at Lily and say, "Lily nudging me to start journaling, guiding my early writing." I turn and address each one at the table. "Mary, your comments from early on, and helping with the structure of the book have been invaluable. Sophie, so patient, yet firm. I learned the importance of a deadline, your guidance, your red pen, and your *connections*—it all made a world of difference. Steven, you have always supported my dreams, letting me bounce ideas off you. So, thanks. To Emily, Lauren, and Alyssa too, you all played a part, you don't know it, but you really did. And Ben, you've taught me the most important lesson, 'to thine own self be true'."

I add, "That reminds me of a t-shirt I saw last week. I think it sums up that sentiment in an interesting way. It said, 'I follow, dot dot dot, me'. I love the simplicity of it. I think today people are following what others are doing and thinking. Social media has people my age focused on everyone else. They don't take the time to listen to themselves."

I raise my glass and say, "To friends."

The first of five courses on the tasting menu is soon brought out. I talk with Sophie about her current projects, and her daughter's recent dance recital. She asks me to take a lot of pictures on my next walk. She says, "I have an idea."

Mary leans forward and says, "I didn't thank you for the acknowledgment in your book."

"Absolutely," I say. "You're the one who got this whole thing rolling."

The chatter continues as the plates keep coming. A new bottle of wine is brought out and shared by all with each course. The menu, delicious, and everything is plated just so.

Steven turns to me and says, "I'm excited to hear about your upcoming trip. I'm still in awe of your last. We need to talk about what to do with the advance from your publisher."

I say with a smile, "Just transfer to my account for now." I'm still surprised they paid me ten grand up front.

"When you return from your trip, I'd like to sit down and discuss your book, and any other endeavors you may be thinking about for the future."

"I'd like that," I say with a smile. "I'll be back the second week of September." Then I add, "Hey, I think Lauren did the right thing last year, traveling. I think you should encourage her to do it again this summer." I know he wasn't thrilled about her going last time, but I want to express my honest opinion.

"I'm open to it," he says, surprising me.

"She seems excited about her new major."

"Yes, I see that too," he says. "I hope this time it sticks."

It's after 10:00 pm when Ben settles the check. Before leaving our table, we all thank him for his generosity. Outside on the street, hugs are shared by all. Steven and this family head to their car; Lily, Ben, and Mary wait for an Uber; Sophie lives only a few blocks away; I start walking on my two-mile trek home. I need to start walking more than just my afternoon stroll with the dogs, if I want to be in shape for my next trek.

I'm feeling loose, my mind dancing; the wine has done its trick. My confidence is at an all-time high. I walk upright, making eye contact with more than a few girls I see. A slight smirk on my face as I pass by.

I walk into the kitchen. Lily is in her pajamas with a bottle in hand.

"So, Jack, did you enjoy your first celebratory dinner where you were the honoree?"

"I did," I say, smiling big. "It's amazing how many people helped make it happen."

"You know, it was *every* person in your life, not just those at dinner."

I know what she means by that. "Yes," I say, nodding, smiling to myself and thinking of my mom.

"It's quite an accomplishment," she says. "I remember how proud Charles was after he finished his first book."

"Yeah, it feels great," I say with a self-assured smile. "I am proud of myself, too."

"You should be," she says. "But remember to stay humble."

She pours us each a glass of Prosecco. Then she raises hers and says, "To love."

I think, an interesting toast, then raise my glass, "To love."

We share a muted smile.

I think about all the people in my life whom I love. Their faces flash in my head. I realize this number has grown substantially over the past year. My eyes well up, my throat tightens as my gratitude sticks in my throat.

NINETEEN / sauna

June 12 –   Oulu, Finland

I walk out of the train station in Oulu, surprised by how bright it is. It's after 10:00 pm. I try to match each face I see to the picture on my phone.

"Mathias?" I say, somewhat hesitantly, to a taller-than-expected man; a blue-eyed blonde.

"Hei, Jack," he says with a smile. Hei pronounced hey, Finnish for hello.

"Hei," I reply.

I follow him to his car, parked just a few steps away.

"Do you speak any Finnish?" He asks.

"Just a few words. This is my first time here."

"Marika (his wife) said you'll be walking the Camino de Santiago."

"Yes, I'm starting in Munich."

"That is a looong way."

"I can't walk the whole thing. I'll probably get to Switzerland and jump ahead."

"That will be some walk." As he pulls onto the street, he says, "It's only a fifteen-minute drive."

"I appreciate you coming to get me—and putting me up."

"My mom told me, any friend of Lily's, is like family here."

"Lily said that your dad and Charles worked together."

"Yes, but they were like family growing up. Even now, my mom and Lily must talk twice a week."

"I didn't know that."

We are driving through a forest, along a two-lane road. The sun's rays make it through the trees and form stripes of light in the road ahead. Ten minutes into the ride, Mathias turns onto a narrower, paved road.

"We're headed to my parent's lake house. My wife, daughter, and I are up for the week. But there is plenty of room. You will be sleeping in the grandkid's room."

I didn't realize they were having their family here too. Now I feel as though I'm intruding. "I'll be sure to stay out of your way."

"No, please join us. It will be fun," he says sincerely.

"Thanks, I appreciate that."

He turns into the drive of a sleekly designed home, and parks in a carport. I grab my pack, a few pounds lighter this time around. I've replaced a few items. Both my bivy and sleeping bag are new, and ounces lighter. Plus, no water filter, or books to weigh it down.

I follow him to the front door.

"I can't believe that's all you're carrying. It looks too small to carry everything you'll need for three months," he says. "I pack light, but that's impressive."

We're greeted at the front door by Emilia. I've seen her picture every day; a framed photo of her and Lily smiling on a beach sits on a living room shelf. I'd recognize her anywhere. She, too, is taller than I expect, matching my five feet ten. Her hair, white, is cut in a bob. Her smile is broad and her teeth a radiant white.

"Hello, Jack. I can't believe we are finally meeting. I've heard so much about you," she says. "I'm so glad Lily convinced you to come."

"Me too. And thanks for having me."

"Absolutely," she says. "Let me give you a hug."

We embrace. Her squeeze is tighter than I expect.

"I normally don't hug someone I just met, but I feel I already know you, from everything Lily has said."

I turn and find an outstretched hand, very tan. "It is nice to meet you. I'm Johannes." His grip is firm.

"Same here," I say. "Thanks for your generosity."

I hold up my pack, "Where should I put this?"

"There are hooks behind you," Emilia says. I turn and see a dozen large pegs in two neat lines, and a long row of cubbies below.

I hang up my pack and place my Chaco sandals in an empty square. I see a woman and child walk into the room.

For the first time, I take in the space I've entered. It's a huge open room. Light wood covers every wall. The vaulted ceiling is covered in the same light wood and climbs to twenty feet; it runs the room's width. Recessed lights softly fill the room. To my left is a large kitchen, the appliances running along one wall. Open shelving above, along with two cabinet doors. Under and over cabinet lighting makes the wall glow with a soft yellow light, reflecting off the birch cabinets and shelves. The backsplash is blue, the same color as their flag, which gives a little pop of color to this monochromatic space. It feels like I just walked into a catalog.

In the center of the room, a large rectangular table with twelve simple chairs—all in a similar light wood. There must be ten feet between the table and a huge island, topped with what looks like a soft white sanded stone.

On the other side of the dining table is a seating area; three large couches form a "U" shape and look out towards a glass wall. Floor to ceiling windows run the width, except for a wide folding door. I look out to a hazy purple sky, the sun having just set. A lake, calm as can be, enhances the view. It is a stunning space. Think Ralph Lauren.

"This is my wife, Marika," Mathias says.

I reach out and shake her hand.

"I'm so happy to meet you," she says. "I read your book; Lily sent us a copy. I loved it."

"Thanks," I say with a smile. "And who is this?" I ask, squatting down on the hardwood floor to get at eye level with a beautiful little girl, her hair so light and fine it's almost white. Her eyes the same deep blue as her parents.

"I'm Jack."

"Hei, my name is Ayden," she says with a sly smile.

"I have a lot planned for the next few days," Emilia says. "Tomorrow we are going sailing on a nearby lake." She says the lake's name, but it's indecipherable to me.

"That sounds like fun."

I look around the house again. "Your house is amazing."

"We have two more boys and their wives and four more grandkids. So, it is a full house on the holidays or whenever everyone can make it up here," Emilia says. "You will be in the bunk room. So, you will see where most everyone sleeps when we are all here."

Soon, I say, "I need to get to bed, it's been a long day." I think everyone stayed up to welcome me, and they're normally asleep by now. Ayden is yawning. It's now pitch black.

"Let me show you to your room," Emilia says. I grab my pack and follow her in my bare feet, the floors radiating heat.

"Good night," I say to the rest.

Emilia points to the bunk room and says, "You'll be in here." The room while not big, has eight neatly made beds, each bunk looks as if it were built into the wall. She opens the door to a large white and blue bathroom. It looks almost commercial: three shower stalls, three sinks, three W.C.'s (or water closet, the European term for a toilet). "If you need to shower tonight, feel free. Breakfast is at eight. I hope you sleep well."

"Thanks," I say. "Good night."

When my head hits the pillow, I know I'll be asleep in minutes. I feel both a sense of excitement for the coming week and gratitude for this family opening their home to me. My eyes feel heavy, my body needs sleep.

After breakfast, a tasty "porridge" with berries, its texture like rice pudding, the six of us load into two cars, heading to yet another lake house. I get in the backseat of a Volvo with Emilia and Johannes.

"We're heading to our friends place," Emilia tells me. "They are back home in Helsinki. They knew we had company, and insisted we go for a sail."

"That was nice," I say. "How often do you come up to *your* place?"

"Maybe twice a month," she says. "We both enjoy being home in Helsinki."

"I keep busy there," Johannes says. "But I love coming up here, just not every week."

"Do you have a big house in Helsinki, too?"

"No. We live in a one-bedroom, eighty-five meters. Like a small apartment in the States," Emilia tells me.

"Really?" I say, surprised.

"We don't need much space, it's just the two of us." she says, "but it's very nice, and on the water."

Our drive keeps us in the same forest I entered just minutes from the train station. I tell them about my time since I moved to Madison.

"Johannes taught there for twenty years," she tells me. "I love it there."

"I did too," Johannes says, "but, we both wanted to get back home. All our family is here now."

"Mathias told me that you talk to Lily often," I say looking at Emilia, "I didn't realize that you were that close."

"She's been one of my best friends for almost fifty years. We grew very close in those early years. For a long time, we'd see each other every year. Us going there, or them coming here. It had been a few years, with Charles's illness. I'm so glad she made it last year."

Johannes tells me, "Charles and I used to go on a long trek whenever we got together. We would take the train and head to the mountains for a few days whenever they visited. It was our way of relaxing."

"He was quite the outdoorsman," Emilia says. "Lily and I liked it when we'd meet somewhere warm. Greece was our favorite."

"I think it's great you all stayed so close," I say, smiling.

"When Lily told me she wasn't up to visit this year, I was disappointed," Emilia says, "And we can't make it there until next summer."

I feel guilty for not knowing she was hoping to visit. I ask, "Did she say why?"

Emilia looks over at her husband, then says, "Only that she was feeling a little tired."

That too a surprise.

Johannes punches a code to the front door, and we enter. It's much smaller than their place, but the view out the back is beautiful. Everything is so green; the lawn, the trees surrounding the lake, and the small patches of grass every fifty meters encircle a lake several times larger than theirs. The sky is blue, the dark water a little choppy.

Soon I'm in a nice size sailing boat that could easily seat six. I'm with Mathias and Marika, as Ayden wanted to sail with "pappa."

This is only my third time sailing; the others were with Mary and the Hoofers. I am only along for the ride, but I learn much more this time. I help pull the ropes when asked, and occasionally take the tiller. The wind blows my hair, the spray in my face. I feel the power as we slice through the water. The wind is so much stronger than on my previous sails. I love it.

After an hour, we drop anchor and jump into *shockingly* cold water. When I surface, I yelp loudly. It takes me a few long minutes to get used to the water, but, it's a refreshing way to start the day. Twenty minutes later, we get back into our boats and make a couple more lake crossings before we head back to shore.

It was a great morning. I'd do it again tomorrow.

Like Mathias said last night, everyone treats me "like family."

I enjoy a lazy afternoon of reading. I found an English edition of Dostoyevsky's, *The Idiot,* on a small bookshelf in the bunk room. I am also introduced to the very Finnish characters, the "Moomins." They're trolls, but think of a friendly cartoon rhino. Ayden loves them.

Marika approaches me as I'm lying on a couch. "Would you like something to drink before dinner? We're having milk, but Johannes is having a beer."

"I'll have a beer. Thanks," I say, thinking milk an unusual choice.

I put my book down and take a seat at the island.

Johannes hands me a bottle. "You'll have to try Salmiakki. It's a Finnish alcohol. Maybe after dinner."

"I will," I say, curious.

Marika pours four glasses of milk. The glasses are well designed—simple with clean lines and are a beautiful shade of a translucent blue. There must be twenty identical glasses of varying sizes on an open shelf, with dozens of white plates and bowls stacked nearby.

Emilia sees me staring at a glass, then says, "These are very Finnish, a classic. They've been around for generations. Kartio by iittala."

"They look so modern."

"They are beautiful, and yet practical. They last forever, which is a very Finnish thing," she says. "Having lived in the States and the Netherlands, I know what is classically Finnish. But all Scandinavian design is the harmony of purpose and form."

Johannes adds, "We will buy something that will last, even if it costs more. If not, you will pay more in the end."

"That is true," Marika says. "The jumper Ayden is wearing has been handed down countless times."

I'm impressed by the practicality of items like these that are built to last. A quality I've not often found in most of the things I've encountered in my life.

I sit next to Johannes at dinner. The main course is a delicious creamy salmon chowder, accompanied by a crusty rye bread. Johannes asks me about my walk last year. I give a quick recap. When I mention my visit to Nathalie's community, and how they lived, he says, "I don't see the attraction in that. That's too much for me."

I think about his comments and decide that I may feel the same way if I had a place like this.

"What do you do for work?" He asks.

I am hesitant to simply say, unemployed, as he is a distinguished professor. "I was a student, and I may be going back, I'm not sure. I like writing, but I doubt I can make a career out of it. So, I am still searching."

I see Johannes's eyes widen, and his brow furrow when I say "searching."

He responds quickly, "Happiness is not found by searching, but by living."

My eyes light up, and I say, "I love that quote."

"It is a Finnish saying."

"I will remember that one."

After dinner, I help Marika with the dishes while the others play a game at the table. Marika is beautiful; straight blond hair hangs just past her shoulders; she wears no makeup; her full lips expose pristine teeth.

"Are you excited for your adventure?" she asks smiling.

"Yeah," I say as I lather a plate. "I had such a good time last year. I'm excited to meet more new people, and I love walking all day."

"I get it," she says. "Mathias could bike all day, that's his passion."

"What's yours?" I ask.

She thinks for a few seconds, then says, "I used to love to sketch. I drew all the time back in school, but lately I have focused on Ayden." Then she adds, "We draw together sometimes. I like that. But, like you, I love to travel. When I was at university, I traveled solo all around the world, usually couchsurfing."

"I don't know what that is."

"It's where locals invite travelers into their home."

"Is it free?"

"Yes, but normally I'd bring a small gift."

"What were some of the favorite places you visited?"

"So many, but I loved Thailand … and Australia," she says, then tells me more about her adventures.

When the dishes are done, we join the others.

An hour later, Emilia says, "Time for the sauna."

I head to the bunk room and find a white towel on my bed. I was told I didn't need a suit.

I strip and wrap myself in the towel, and wait for Emilia. We're the last two out.

We exit out a side door, just past my room and the bath in the hall, and onto the deck. We walk toward a small gray-sided square.

"Jack, I've waited to tell you, so as not to have you stew. You're American, so this may be a shock, but we'll all be nude. Feel free to join us or keep your towel wrapped."

She's right, I am surprised. A second later, she pulls the door open, before I decide. Centered on a bench, Marika, staring back.

Gulp.

I *join* them and take a seat near the door. My awkwardness lasts only for a few long seconds. I remain quiet, remembering the last time I was nude in front of mixed company; skinny-dipping in Rest Lake when I was on staff at camp. Soon we're all talking and my comfort level returns to normal, well almost.

One topic of conversation tonight, here in the heat—public saunas. They are very popular in the larger Finnish cities where titles and class are literally all stripped away. Everyone is equal, in a way, as the sexes combine.

"It's one of the rare places in our society where everyone mixes," Johannes says. "While it is encouraged to talk with strangers, staying silent is fine, but you must avoid controversial topics like politics."

"That's smart."

"The sauna is good for the body, and the mind," Mathias tells me.

I see birch branches in the corner of the room, and ask, "What are those for?"

"They're used to renew your skin. You whack them all over your body," Marika says.

"Interesting," I say. "Maybe I'll try that tomorrow."

After twenty minutes, I follow the rest and we walk down the lawn and onto a small pier. One by one we jump into the cold, cold void.

We repeat this cycle two more times, then head back inside.

The next morning Emilia invites me to join her for a swim.

I put my suit on.

She is wearing one too. Phew.

We swim slowly around the lake. It is eerily quiet, and everything is still. The only sounds, the ripple of the water as we glide and a bird's wings flapping overhead. We slow every few minutes, to ask or answer a question.

When we get to the far side of the lake, Emilia treads water, looks at me and says, "Lily sent me a text last night." She smiles. "She wanted me to share some good news with you. The *State Journal* just published a *glowing* review of your book."

My eyes bulge. My jaw drops.

"Wow," I say. "I wasn't expecting that." I'm shocked. I think to myself, how? It's got to be Sophie. I smile, my heart warms with gratitude.

"Congratulations, Jack," she says, with her beautiful smile.

In the afternoon, I'm invited to join the men on the golf course. Being unsure of their abilities, but knowing mine, I pass on their offer. I don't want to embarrass myself and slow them down. Instead, I join the women on a bike ride.

"You can take Mathias's old road bike," Marika says.

I hop on, and balance by my toes. I lower the seat. My feet, now, rest flat.

"I didn't think you'd want to ride Johannes's old Jopo."

"Jopo's are a perfectly fine bike," Emilia says from atop hers.

"Another Finnish Classic," she says with a grin. "I've always had one."

"But yours is only half the age of dads."

Emilia laughs and says, "Yes, he's had it for forty years. But it still rides fine."

The four of us slowly head into Oulu, Ayden leads the way. A dedicated path is paved all the way to town. Our first stop, the library. It's stunning, made almost entirely of glass. Next, we pick up groceries and stop for coffee before heading back.

The next few days are filled with more swimming, reading, biking, and games. Some of us go on hikes, one in the forest, another through a marsh on wobbly planks. We also go sailing again. Yay!

My time to leave comes, and I'm ready. Excited for my journey by foot.

Emilia drives me to the train station for my five-hour trip to Helsinki. Tomorrow, I fly to Munich.

"Thanks for everything," I say as we share a hug.

I grab my pack, and walk inside to my train that's already here, waiting.

> *I want to talk about everything with at least one person as I talk about things with myself.*
>
> Fyodor Dostoyevsky, *The Idiot*

TWENTY / surf

June 21 –   Munich, Germany

I walk along a well-marked path on the outskirts of Munich; the excitement to be on another adventure shows on my face. I left my hostel just after the sun started its climb. While the sky was bright for most of the morning, the sky is now overcast. My accommodations for tonight are still unknown. I had planned to walk until dusk and find a place outside, but the sky worries me. A night in the rain would not be a good start. I decide to try couchsurfing, having downloaded the app after talking with Marika.

In my Couchsurfing bio, I explain my walking life. I send requests to three members in the town of Starnberg, twenty-eight kilometers from today's starting point. My only requirement is that the host speak English. Supposedly, each should message back and advise if I can stay.

I walk on, fingers crossed, as the sky darkens.

Half an hour later, my phone pings. A message reads, "Sorry, but I'm not in town."

I feel disheartened, but I still have two more chances, though I envision a night in the rain. I look up and pray.

Another ping, another "sorry." I march on. The clouds grow more ominous.

I reach the town, my destination, and sit outside a bar at a picnic table. I order a beer when the waiter comes, my answer "large" when given a choice in size. A minute later an oversized mug arrives. With its thick glass, and being filled to the brim, its weight surprises.

An elderly man, with a thick mustache, points to a bench opposite me.

I nod my head, and say, "Of course."

He speaks some English. We chat about the weather for a minute, and then he nods towards my pack.

"Are you traveling?"

"Yes. I am walking a very long way."

His questions keep coming. I learn he's here on holiday.

"This is a resort town. People love the lake," he says. "Expensive." He grins.

I know, I had checked for a bed this morning. "Too pricy for me."

This kind man buys me a beer when he orders his next round.

I'm enjoying our conversation when a light rain starts to fall. Umbrellas are extended, keeping us dry for now. My stomach starts to churn; I'm not looking forward to tonight's forested sleep.

My phone pings, yet again. I'm afraid to look.

I take out my phone. It's already after 5:30 pm. I open the app and read the message.

"You are welcome to stay," and lists his address and Apt. 3. "What time will you be here? I am already home," his message reads.

Using Google Maps, I find he's an eight-minute walk away.

I message back, "Fantastic! I'll be there by six."

I try to explain couchsurfing to my drinking partner, but he doesn't understand. I stand, we shake hands and I head into the mist.

Stefan, who looks to be in his late twenties, is dressed in a t-shirt and shorts. He stands in his doorway, smiling. I shake off and remove my pack and rain jacket before entering. It's a small apartment, a studio. I see a blow-up mattress folded on the floor; an electric pump next to it.

"I hope you don't mind sleeping on this."

"No, this is perfect."

"I walked the Camino last year," he tells me. "I started in Saint-Jean-Pied-du-Port."

"That's great. I'm excited to be walking again."

He asks about my walk last year. Later, he says, "I usually don't accept someone who has no reviews, but your story was interesting, plus you're on a Camino. I love getting to know new people."

He offers me dinner and I accept. Macaroni and Cheese, and slices of dense brown bread.

It quells my empty stomach.

We talk for a couple more hours before going to sleep. He on a bed pulled from the couch, me floating on air.

The morning comes. After buttered toast and a glass of orange juice, we head out together. He to work and me into the unknown. Thankfully, the rain has stopped and the sun is out.

Walking out of this small town, I can't stop thinking of last night. The openness and friendliness of Stefan. A conversation with a real German, learning about his life and dreams. If this is typical of couchsurfing—I'm stoked I signed up.

Within half an hour, I decide on what towns I will be passing through around dinner time for each of the next two days. I search out my next possible hosts, but none are listed in the app as I'm headed into a more remote region of Bavaria. So, I walk, head up, taking in the views. Still, the potential for more nights like last night adds to my excitement. I pass a yellow sign that's been hammered onto a small wooden shed, it reads "Santiago 2605km." I do the math, 1618 miles. I really do need to jump ahead. It's either going to be one big leap, or a couple smaller ones. For now, I'll simply walk and embrace each new day.

After a night outside, and a night in a "Pilgerzimmer," which I find is a simple room in someone's home. There is barely any interaction, and no meal is provided, but it's affordable enough. I finally find another couchsurfing opportunity for tonight. Stefan left me a stellar review, making it easier to score another bed. I am headed to Marktoberdorf where a married couple has offered me a place.

Today the views have changed for the better. I make my way over rolling hills along narrow dirt paths, the broad vista of the Austrian Alps to the south have me shaking my head. They look so close, but are actually over thirty kilometers away.

My hosts offer me dinner and a private room. We share our stories and connect. The evening passes quickly, then we head to bed.

These nights with strangers continue, adding to my fun. The landscapes are incredible, but it feels like I'm simply passing the time until I meet the next welcoming soul. While it is not every night, I'm lucky about half the time.

This afternoon I am greeted a block away from my latest host's home.

"Are you Jack?" A boy, maybe ten years old, asks.

"I am," I say with a smile.

"Follow us," he says. Another boy, six, leads the way.

"What are your names?"

"I'm Sam. This is my brother, Ron."

I smile. Ron … my dad's name.

Their mom, Lisa, welcomes me at the front door of their townhome. She gives me a tour and points out my bed, in a small room in the attic.

I shower and change.

When I come back down, we talk, and I look through a few of her scrapbooks. Each one of a different vacation. "I've been to twenty-two countries. Sam has already been to ten."

"How long have you been having guests like me?"

"It's been years. But I've been a guest far more times than we've hosted. It's our way of giving back to the community."

"I think the concept is brilliant," I say.

"We don't travel nearly as much as we did when we were younger. But I find that hosting fills that void. I get to meet new people, which has always been my favorite part."

A while later, her husband Markus arrives home from work. We talk over a beer on their patio while he fires up his grill. Hamburgers and hotdogs are on the menu. "The boys love hotdogs."

We enjoy an al fresco dinner, and more beer as we talk about our lives. It's another conversation-filled night. I love learning about others' lives, and even more, I enjoy sharing mine.

In the morning, after her kids head to school, Lisa takes me on a bicycle tour of her city. We stop near a pond, which I learn acts as a public pool. I count eight people swimming laps. Ninety minutes later, we're back at her home. I grab my pack and resume my walk; again, I shake my head at the kindness I've received.

Two days later, I must race to yet another anticipated stay. I get a late start and need to cover over thirty-five kilometers. I walk at a faster-than-normal pace to arrive at our agreed to time. The scenery is lovely, and I even walk up on a deer. I get within ten feet, and still it remains, our eyes locked. I am surprised by the calmness of this creature, it's beauty. I stop. Finally, he looks down and continues his meal. I stroll on; another memory made.

Lina, who looks to be about thirty, shows up with two bags of groceries just minutes after I arrive. I take a bag and we walk upstairs to her apartment on the second floor. She points out the bathroom and says, "You can shower in there." Then we walk into her living space, and she says, "You'll be sleeping on the couch. These cubes," which look like stools, "will turn it into a bed."

"Great," I say. I set down my pack and look at photos hanging on the walls while she unpacks her groceries.

A couple of minutes later, I say "I think I'll shower now, if that's okay."

"Yes. I'm sure it's been a long day."

I grab my relatively clean town clothes, my travel towel, and head into the bathroom. I hurriedly rinse off and wash my hair. Looking in the mirror, I stare at my face. It's tan and I have about a week's worth of a beard—it looks pretty good.

I join Lina in the small kitchen and sit at small table with two chairs.

"Would you like a drink? I have some wine."

"Wine would be great."

She hands me the bottle and a corkscrew, and says, "Can you open it? I'm making pasta, and a salad for dinner."

"Wow, thanks, that's perfect."

It takes me a few minutes, but finally I have two glasses poured.

"Here's to couchsurfing and meeting new people," I say.

We clink glasses, and each take a sip.

"It's good," I say.

"In Germany, we say, "Prost.""

I raise my glass again. Together we toast as we look each other in the eye.

Before we start the salad, I empty the bottle by refilling our glasses.

"Don't worry, I have more."

We enjoy dinner at the small table, talking about travel and our couchsurfing experiences. Her smile expands when she tells me about her love of music; she plays the violin for a local orchestra. She brings out a second bottle after we finish eating, moving to the couch to continue our conversation.

After thirty minutes of talking and listening to music. I stare at her, my eyes heavy with drink. I want to kiss her. I reach out and touch her thigh.

Her mouth opens slightly. She looks down at my hand and gently lifts it away. She shakes her head, her expression serious.

Apparently, I've misread the situation. We have been talking for hours and I thought there was a romantic connection. It must have been my imagination, that something in her eyes and expression said to approach. I think I catch a slight smirk. I decide she's playing hard to get.

***

I wake. My mouth dry. My head throbbing.

A memory flashes—embarrassment fills my head.

Light flows in through a sheer curtain. I sit up. I look at my phone. It's after 8:00 am.

I stand and see a note.

"You can see yourself out."

My stomach starts to churn. I start to sweat. What a fool I am.

I leave the empty apartment within minutes of waking.

I find my blue line and walk quickly—escaping the scene of my crime.

My mind races as I attempt to piece last night together.

Knowing whatever happened, was my fault.

As I walk, flashes appear, and my embarrassment grows.

Acting cocky. Bragging. Then begging—until she says, "No … it's not going to happen." She gets up from the couch and says, "Goodnight." Her tone curt.

Her door closes before I pass out.

Drinking too much, a habit I thought I'd broken.

That me who was lost, has returned.

I play loud rock and roll music, trying to drown out a voice that won't let me go.

This continues for hours. No food, only water. I push myself; I do not stop.

The landscape is amazing, though it barely registers.

My day ends in the dark, in a forest alone.

The voice relents, allowing me to sleep.

Raskolnikov enters my dreams.

His crime: murder. His punishment—eight years hard labor comes only after he confesses.

My crimes are many: pride, gluttony, and definitely lust.

My punishment still awaits.

I wake, but the torment remains.

As I walk this morning, I think back to previous painful episodes in my life. Realizing now, I will do anything to avoid thinking about the root of my pain. To this day, it's hard to talk about my dad without tears—so I don't. Then, as I'm failing out of college, rather than deal with it, I ignore it, blow off finals and take a road trip. I've always sought out something exciting—anything but dwell on the shard of glass causing me pain.

I download Raskolnikov's story and listen from dawn to dusk.

It's not meant to distract. I walk in my pain, my mind working to find answers.

My actions have shown I am not who I thought.

Lessons learned in the past—I must have forgot.

Have I become the person I've always detested? An arrogant prick.

I wake on day three, back in the woods.

Selfishly, I check to see if she's left a review.

Grateful, she says only, "He was a good guest."

I spend the morning drafting my regret.

> *Lina –*
> *I apologize for not contacting you sooner. I want to say I'm sorry for my actions. Your openness and generosity showed who you are, while my attitude and actions showed the real me. I'm not who I thought I was when I first walked through your door. I truly enjoyed our evening, until I went too far. You deserved far better, more than just my respect. Forgiveness is not what I seek. Please know that I have thought about that night and will work to become a better person.*
> *Sincerely, Jack*

I click send.

This afternoon I reach the town of Lindau which sits on the German side of a lake named Constance.

I hop on a ferry and decide on a plan.
The only requirement: to reach Santiago before my visa expires.
I step off onto a new land—Switzerland.
I leave Germany behind, or at least I try to.
Though forgiving myself is not yet near, my head is starting to clear.
My life in solitary continues.
Two train rides, and I am in Lausanne.
A night in a familiar locale, reassures.
I take a night swim, attempting to wash it away.
Rightfully so, the stain remains.
Putting a country between me and my sin.
Tomorrow I'll be in France once again.

> *The man who has a conscience suffers whilst acknowledging his sin. That is his punishment.*
>
> Fyodor Dostoyevsky,
> *Crime and Punishment*

TWENTY-ONE / the way

July 5 –   Le Puy-en-Velay, France

Sitting in the cathedral in the town of Le Puy, just after 7:00 in the morning. I look around the church, still dim, but an early morning sun attempts to brighten the space as its rays shine through stained glass perched high above the altar. Ancient gray stone columns flank the wooden pews. I listen to the priest, though, I am uncertain what is being said. Thirty or so other pilgrims surround me, our packs lined up, ready to go. I have already gotten the first stamp in my new "Credencial del Perigrino," what the French call the Pilgrim's Passport. I bought it yesterday in a shop near where I now sit.

At the end of the service, a blessing is offered, said in French and English for the pilgrims making their journey along "the Way." The priest wishes us a "bon chemin," meaning a safe walk along the road to Santiago. Just then, the floor between the two columns of pews starts to drop, and it becomes a stairway heading down. I look on in astonishment—it is quite the feat. We exit en masse, headed towards Santiago de Compostela, over fifteen hundred kilometers away.

I purchased a guidebook called the *Miam Miam Dodo* yesterday. The title is French child-speak meaning "yum, yum" and "nighty night." Besides maps for each "stage," it lists all the places you can eat and sleep for the next seven hundred and thirty-six kilometers; all the way to Saint-Jean-Pied-du-Port. The book is in French, which is fine since it has symbols for everything, but I'm disappointed that I've lost the French I'd gained on last year's walk.

Once I make my way out of town, I slow my pace when I catch up to a pilgrim about my age. She wears glasses, a pink floppy hat, and carries an oversized pack, twice the size of mine.

"That looks heavy," I say, with an astonished smile.

"It is," she says. "I haven't walked with it before, or at least not once it was fully packed. I'm nervous."

I find she is from Paris and is walking to Santiago, too. She tells me, "Most people that start here are French. Many will stop in Saint-Jean, but most will stop long before. Most are long-distance trekkers on holiday, not pilgrims. But they, too, will need a passport to stay in some of the lodgings along the way."

Later, we catch up to a mother and son. We walk together for some time talking about what led us here. The boy, twelve, complains about his feet.

"It's my fault," his mom says, "the guy who sold us his boots said we should get the next size up, but it was a men's size, and cost thirty euros more. I was being cheap."

The boy is clearly not happy. I don't blame him, getting blisters on day one would suck. His mom says, "I know you're in pain, but I am too. My shoulders are killing me." She explains that because she feels bad about his shoes, she took stuff from his pack and added it to hers. "I thought this would be an adventure we could share."

"It's bound to get better," I say hopefully.

We say goodbye to the uncomfortable pair and continue on at our faster pace.

When the common stopping point for the first stage nears, my Parisienne friend says, "I'm going to stop here."

We are standing next to a small clearing, about a kilometer from the village where I hope to stay.

"I plan on sleeping in my tent most nights," she says. "I don't have money to pay for a place that often."

We stop and drop our packs. She digs out a tent. It alone, almost as big as my loaded pack, and then a sleeping bag that looks like it would keep her warm in the middle of winter. She rolls out her tent; it can easily sleep four.

As she sets it up, I tell her, "I sleep outside sometimes too, but only in a lightweight bag that packs up into the size of a one-liter bottle."

"I'll keep going with what I have for now."

Ten minutes later, I say, "J'espère the revoir." I hope to see you again.

Reaching the village of Montbonnet, I find a bed at "Gîte La 1ère étape", the first stage hostel.

Like the lodgings along the Via Francigena, I share a room with nine others.

In the morning, our hosts offer breakfast and help adjust their guests' packs.

The mother from yesterday expresses relief, learning now what I learned last year, how to carry the weight on her hips.

"I knew that, but I didn't tell you," her son says bitterly, "because of my boots." Yikes!

Mom shakes her head. "I will buy you new ones when we find a place. I promise."

With that, I'm off. Solo again.

The route takes me along quiet gravel paths, through rolling hills covered with trees. Then through small villages, and next to fields with ancient stone walls, through gated pastures where cows mind their own business, heads down munching on grass. Soon, another village where I find food, then continue. This pattern repeats for days on end.

My lodgings are mostly gîtes, with shared rooms and shared meals. Most I meet are walking in pairs, and I seldom see the same face twice, as my pace is faster than most.

While the landscape and the charming ancient villages are more stunning than on my walk through France last year, my excitement is muted. I miss the camaraderie I felt along my walk last year.

I push on alone, my mind finally free to think and not dwell.

I consciously change my mindset, forcing myself to smile. I haven't been the same since that regretful night. Before then, I felt as though I was near my peak. How quickly I fell from that selfish delusion. I now must focus, and practice being the person I want to become.

The days pass more joyfully and soon the gratitude for the life I'm living returns.

Finally, I reach the outskirts of Saint-Jean-Pied-du-Port before the sun is at its peak. I head to an office to gather the information I need. The first ones I meet, three missionaries who've made vows to God. A sign? What does it mean?

Tomorrow, I will climb over the Pyrenees. Today, I take a much-needed rest.

I barely saw a soul along my route in the last week, now, I walk along cobbled streets and pass a never-ending stream of smiling faces. I assume most are here to begin their journey to Santiago de Compostela and the remains of Jesus' disciple James. This town is a common starting point for the Camino de Santiago.

Logistically, this walk should be a piece of cake. I have a spreadsheet listing the accommodations from here to the end. Tons of options it seems, but a simple bed is all I need.

Friends are made along the way, walking all day in a group. We find places to stay, though it's crowded. The nights are fun, sharing our lives over bottles of wine. I *am* careful to remain who I should be.

The walk is mostly flat, though we do have a few tough climbs. It's August and the sun intensifies the heat. Each afternoon becomes a struggle; it forces a change. Now up at 5:00 am, and napping during the hottest part of each day. When I reach the city of Burgos, one of the largest on the Camino, I decide to get my hair cut short, the sides almost shaved. I like it, I'm surprised; my long hair has always been a part of me.

There are days I walk solo, as my pace exceeds that of new friends. Today is an example, as they stop, I continue to the small village of Grañón.

I arrive at a church and find the door to the alberque (pronounced al·**bear**·gay) around back. Albergue is the Spanish term for a pilgrim's hostel. I find there are no beds, only forty mats. Dinner is a communal affair, with everyone pitching in. The room is filled with those from distant lands, ten countries in all. Half are Italian, and they volunteered to prepare our main course. Our dinner is delicious: soup, salad, and pasta with a tasty homemade sauce. Later in the church's loft, we gather. The lights go out, and a candle is lit. It passes to each pilgrim and we all share something meaningful the Camino has brought.

"Sharing this journey with others, despite starting out alone, has made my walk more meaningful as new friends are made," is what I say. I listen intently to the others. Their experiences move me and tears start to flow. As I sit in the dark, this evening ingrains and forgiveness is sought.

My Camino continues, and I search for more nights like Grañón. Together, with others, sharing a meal and a piece of ourselves. My walking partners change as I continue my pace. The Meseta, Spain's wide swath of flat and endless plains, arrives. My night in San Anton, an ancient convent with no electricity, ranks high on my list of memorable stays.

It is here where twelve strangers gather in ruins, again, there is no roof. A campfire blazes … wine is passed … a guitar comes out, though I do not play … we sing together, and each share a bit of our story … for hours we sit as the stars shine down… memories are made.

As the kilometers pass, my connection to this place grows. The Camino is something new, like my walk to Rome, but here it is something *more*. Those I meet, like me, are at a crossroads, unsure where our life's path will lead. The longer I walk, the more pilgrims I meet walking this same path for the second, third, or in one case, a sixth time. I'm told it's addictive. I get it. I find there are a dozen paths across Spain, all heading to the remains of Saint James. Most I meet are not religious, though I hear "spiritual" often.

Me—I am not religious. I haven't attended church in quite a while, though I learned the basics in Sunday School in my early days. For the last couple of years, I like to think of kindness as my religion. Though now, having lost myself for a minute, on that night not long ago, I am starting to question what I am. Spiritual? I don't know what it means. Yes, I think there is something greater looking down. For me it's my dad, the higher power I seek to please. Anything more, I am unsure.

 On this journey across Spain, everyone walks to connect—to themselves and others. The Camino de Santiago is a dream, all of it, the crowds, the heat, the snorer next to you at night. The feeling here—unique.

Today, August 25th, I am staying at an albergue in Villafranca del Bierzo. According to the last signpost I passed we are a hundred and seventy-seven kilometers away from Santiago. For the last week, I have been walking with the same group of four others. We've formed a "Camino family," and range in age from eighteen to fifty-two. We walk in smaller groups during the day, but always find ourselves together each evening.

After checking into the albergue, we make our way down to the river and jump in. The waterway is slowed by a dam like wall. The chilled water is invigorating on this blistering afternoon. We lay in the sun and dry in minutes. We soon head into the heart of the city. The five of us are sipping cold beer on a patio overlooking the village square, and laughing about a particularly loud snorer last night, when my phone pings. I see a text from Mary. "Please call me." It's the middle of the night in Madison. I'm surprised. She never texts me. My heart races.

"Excuse me," I say to my friends, "I have to make a call."

I walk to a quiet spot away from the crowds.

After two rings, Mary answers. "Hi Jack. I have terrible news. Lily passed away in the night."

My breath leaves my body. As Mary talks, my spatial awareness, like an Etch-a-Sketch being shaken, vanishes. After I hang up, I have difficulty remembering everything she said. I lean against a stone wall and close my eyes; they fill with tears. I take a few slow breaths. Realizing my walk is over, I accept it. I need to find my way back home.

I walk back and take my seat.

"Are you okay?"

"A good friend of mine passed away," I say solemnly.

Soon, we all head back to our albergue where dinner is offered. Robotically, I go through the motions until I lay in my top bunk for the night. Once all my travel home is booked, I stare at a heavy wooden beam. In my mind, I see Lily smiling at me outside the coffee shop, then in the kitchen asking about my day. I think of the picture of her with her horse, her dream, unfulfilled. Again, I feel my eyes start to well, but I blink away the tears. Then I let out a sound; it's part laugh, part sob, when a memory pops into my head. I open the front door and find Lily singing and dancing to Abba's *Dancing Queen*. Her spinning around, then she sees me standing there. She and I both burst out laughing. I will miss her.

Then, selfishly, I ponder what Lily's death means for me. My mind races about what I'll need to do when I get back home. Lily's service, then where do I go, what will I do.

I think of my dad's death. I can't believe it's already been nine years. After he was gone, I was always looking for something to distract me. I'd been running from the pain of losing him for years. It wasn't until I met Lily that I stopped.

Now, like that day two years ago, I am still unsure. Lily provided a haven of sorts, a place to grow, but more importantly, to postpone having to decide what direction I should head. In death, Lily is forcing me to pick a path to follow.

Walk with the knowledge that you are never alone.
—Audrey Hepburn

(Quote found painted on a highway underpass along the Camino de Santiago)

TWENTY-TWO / love

August 29 –   Madison, Wisconsin

On my first night back in Madison, I lie in my bed and try to identify my choices. Move back to my hometown; a step backward, and return to my old high school job, putting off a decision on a long-term plan. Maybe find a cheap apartment in Madison, find a part-time job, *or* ask Steven about that job offer from last year. Vanlife too, is an option, as living outside is appealing, but the endless solitude may be a bit too much.

I will continue to write, no matter where I end up, but finding a place to live is my first hurdle. I think about what I've learned since I was last in this position. I force myself to identify a career path to follow—my best guess on creating a happy life. I spend what feels like an hour exploring a multitude of possibilities in my head. I follow each path years into the future, ruling each out for any number of reasons. I land on one that surprises me. It's something I had not entertained in the past. I want to be a high school English teacher. My mind now clear, I drift into sleep.

I walk from Lily's house to Steven's office, two blocks from the Capitol, under a beautiful blue sky. It feels good to walk again, especially without a pack. I haven't walked the last few days, except when I needed to catch my next train or plane.

Lily's service is tomorrow. I was asked, or should I say instructed, by Lily to give her eulogy. Something I've known since Mary called that night. Lily had left a letter with her final wishes. I spent much of my eight-hour flight working on it, but I am getting more nervous the closer it gets.

Steven and I shake hands, then hug.

"I'm still in shock," I say.

"Me too."

Steven hands me a framed picture of Lily and Charles, from their younger days. It's one I haven't seen before.

"I had it enlarged," he says. "Have you finished writing what you are going to say?"

"Pretty much," I say with my lips downturned.

"Man, they were an attractive couple," I say, while admiring the photo.

"Lily left this for you," he says as he hands me a linen envelope.

The fact that she left me a letter, comes as a surprise. I wonder if she knew.

"Thanks," I say. "I'll see you there tomorrow."

"Yes. And thank you for coming to get this."

Mary shared with us that Lily asked for a few tasteful photos from her life to be displayed at her service. Steven said he had one she loved, the one I'm holding. I found two others that Lily had hanging in her room; one with her parents when she was a child, and the other of her with a horse when she was in her twenties. Mary left a large, framed photo on the kitchen table. The photo is of a middle-aged Lily. She looks stunning, a serious expression and a glint in her eye. I love it.

When I reach an intersection, I can go right towards campus or straight to get home. I go right. On the Union's patio, I look out at the sailboats on this beautiful day. I open the envelope with "Jack" written in *her* hand.

Dear Jack –

I know my passing likely comes as a shock to you. I tried my best to keep my condition from you. I'm sorry. I loved seeing the happy-go-lucky, yet serious Jack. You didn't need the burden. I wanted to be a light for you, not a cloud to darken your days. Now, on to what I want to tell you.

Before we met that day, I hoped for something or someone to come into my life, but I didn't know why. When we met, I found the why.

You've been a good friend to me, and to the rest of our circle. I'm so glad you extended it and added much to it.

My last years have been wonderful. Something I didn't think was possible after Charles passed away. I owe that to you.

For the last few years, I have thought about how my estate could best be used. I want it to help people, now and in the future. I want a legacy.

My dear Jack, I know you. I know your heart. I trust you to honor that legacy. I know you will "do good" with this opportunity to create something lasting. Use your imagination.

All my love,
Lily

P.S. Thanks in advance for your beautiful eulogy. It will be excellent practice. I know how you hate public speaking.

I laugh, and tears stream from my face. This is the first time I've really cried since she died. I push back thoughts of going back to school and think of Lily. How can I honor her? How can I ever thank her?

I will be forever grateful to her. She created a nurturing environment for me to grow, and still be me. Because of her, I didn't need to worry about food or shelter. That's huge. Instead, I could focus on finding out what mattered to me.

***

I stand behind the pulpit. I look out to the pews, full, a few more standing in the back of this small church. The vaulted ceiling grows in height as it approaches the altar. I nod to my mom and brothers sitting with those closest to Lily, including Emilia and Johannes.

The large picture of Lily in her prime stands on an easel, next to her coffin. Lily, her hair dark, wears a hint of a smile.

I clear my throat and take a drink of water.

My stomach is in knots.

The first words come.

"Lily was loved."

I pause.

"This I know."

I pause.

"Look at this room. Love. We all loved her."

I pause.

"Last year, I asked her why she invited me into her life. She said she saw a lost soul with a kind smile. She told me she had wanted to make a difference in someone's life."

I pause.

"She was right about the lost soul. When we first met, I had no direction. No map and no destination."

I pause.

"She offered me a space to grow—to think. She lifted me up, so I could get a bird's eye view; helping me find a path to becoming, hopefully, a better human."

I pause.

"I pray I've been worthy of her attention." My voice cracking. "She provided me a simple room, a listening ear, and a gentle nudge—with "you should read this book" or "you might like journaling." She was changing my course with each slight adjustment."

I smile.

"Looking back, I see these little things as clear as day. But in the moment, we were simply having a conversation."

"Subtle—the teacher in her—the therapist."

"Her voice was the wind, filling my sails as I moved towards a destination yet to be discovered."

I pause.

"Love ... Lily radiated it."

I pause.

"I saw love in her eyes when the phone would ring and a familiar name popped up."

"I saw love when she talked about her Charles—her parents."

"I saw love when she smiled at a stranger."

I pause. Tears well in my eyes.

"I saw love ... when she looked at me."

My voice cracking, tears flow. I look at those in the front pews, tears streaming.

"On one of the last evenings we spent together, she raised her glass and said, 'To love'."

I pause.

I call to those in this holy place, "Can we all raise a glass, raise our hearts, and hands—to Lily."

I say, "To love," as I raise my hand, as if holding the stem of a glass. The response, "To love."

"One last request ... it was Lily's. She asked that everyone find one person near you and hug them, as if you were giving *her* one last meaningful embrace."

After learning of Lily's request, I knew exactly who I wanted to share this moment ... Jamie. He lost his dad when he was only six. Then a few years later, I, his oldest brother selfishly deserted our family's home, leaving them to endure on their own. This guilt I still carry.

I walk down from the lectern and hug my youngest brother.

***

Two days later, I'm back in Steven's office.

"Lily had been worried about what to do with her estate since Charles passed. She told me to update things late last year, making you the sole beneficiary." She told me, "I trust Jack to find the best use for it."

My jaw drops.

He explains that her estate consists of the house, investments, the property up north (which I've been to a few times), and a parcel of land about fifteen miles west of here (that I did not know about).

Steven says, "They bought forty acres about thirty years ago, planning someday to build a house and a place where Lily could keep a horse or two. Combined, the real estate alone is worth a few million. All together you're looking at upwards of five. Everything is yours. She wanted no restrictions on what you could do with it."

"Wow," I say, shaking my head. "I don't know what to say." My mouth hangs open.

"She asked me to help in any way I could. Setting up a trust, or whatever you decide. In her letter to me, she mentioned that if there was a project, maybe at some point we could work together," he says. "I'd love to be involved on whatever you decide to do in Lily's honor."

"Yeah. Of course," I say, still in shock.

"You'll need time to process all this. I'll work on changing the title to the properties, and her car. But in the meantime, the house is yours. Lily had said most of the house has been cleaned out pretty good."

"Yes," I say with a nod. Then shake my head at the realization; she must have known for a long time.

"Here are the keys to the lake property. You know the quirks up there," he says, handing me the keys.

"Yeah. I think I might head up there for a while," I say, "to think about things."

"Great idea, Jack," he says with a solemn expression. "Call if you have any questions."

On my walk home, I text Jimmy, *Dinner tonight?*

A minute later, *Absolutely.*

We eat Chinese takeout in Lily's kitchen while I explain everything that has happened. He is surprised to say the least.

"I have no idea what I should do," I say. "I don't feel right about spending her money." I show him the letter she left me.

"Maybe you can start a charity, or an endowment to pay for scholarships," he says.

"Maybe," I say, then tell him my plan to spend time alone and think.

In the morning, I head north.

TWENTY-THREE / reflection

September 6 –   Minocqua, Wisconsin

I look out a large picture window and stare at the blue peeking through the pines. The lake is twenty yards down a gentle slope. Lily's letter, my journal, a blank legal pad, and pen are on the table in front of me.

I smile when I remember Lily saying, "Your life's a blank canvas, Jack. What will you create?"

Then my mind goes back to the day I met her, her smile, my state of mind—yes, a lost soul. What am I now? I feel a bit lost again. My circle of friends here—it was Lily that brought me in. I was only included because of her ... what now, with her gone?

My mind jumps to my time in Finland, and how I haven't really reflected on my time there. As soon as it was over, I was walking again.

Then to *that* night. My shame. Questioning, again, my worthiness of Lily's trust.

My mom. My brothers. My dad.

That night in a castle, ecstasy under the stars. Wow, how lucky I've been.

Along the Via Francigena, when I felt the happiest I'd ever been. Why? Why was I so happy then?

Adventure comes to mind, then just being outside, and the people. Yes, the people.

Then Lily's loss hits me … yet again. I'm alone. Lost. No map. No destination.

The words that my mind just uncovered: Adventure, Outside, People. I write these as headings on the legal pad. These words relate to happiness, at least for me.

What does adventure mean? I think. Something different, out of the ordinary, that's key. Next word that comes to mind is risky, the unknown. Not sure if I'll make it. I write these words down under the adventure heading.

Okay, I move to the outside heading. Nature. Green. Active. Fresh. I list these as well.

People: Together. Share. Community.

I look at what I've written. I am not sure what it is.

Is this supposed to tell me something?

I get up from the table, grab my jacket, and go outside.

I head up the drive to a quiet lane. I've taken this same walk for the past two days. I came up here to think about what I should do. But so far, no ideas.

I get back to the house and finish re-reading the book I started this morning, *The Alchemist*.

I fix dinner, eggs.

I sleep.

In the morning, I fix breakfast, eggs.

I go back to my makeshift desk.

Adventure. Outside. People.

I think back to my first long walk. The people I met, the camaraderie I felt.

I think about Lily and her circle. They welcomed me with open arms.

I think about my family. Love, unconditional. Forgiveness.

I think about my Camino, cut short, and the people I met. I smile. Sharing yourself.

I think about my dad and wonder. Would he be proud?

My mission, assigned by Lily, must be focused on people. I unfold her final letter: "… to help people, now, and in the future."

I look at the legal pad.

I start to connect words in each column.

Outside.

People outside.

People outside in nature together.

Risk.

People in nature. Risk.

Together.

Living together.

Cooperation.

I think of Nathalie's home. The community. I know it's a bit much for some.

I loved it there. The people. The togetherness.

I want *that*!

I want to *share* that.

I want to *live* in that.

Togetherness.

Wow!

My mind races.

How do I create that.

My heart beats faster.

I smile.

This vision seems perfect; But does it honor Lily? Will it help people, or just me?

For now, it's simply an idea I want to explore.

I decide to take a long, long walk and roll things around in my head. I pack a lunch and go. I think about the design, the layout of Nathalie's place. I think of Emilia's home, the beauty, the simplicity. I play with ideas as I move through the trees.

At night, I sketch layouts of a community. Then the living spaces, the options. In the morning, I take a road trip and walk Lily's land … where she dreamed of a life with horses.

The days pass. I find photos online to express what's in my mind. I order books from Amazon.

I dial Nathalie's number.

"Jack?"

"Hello, Nathalie," I say, smiling. "I hope you're doing well."

"Things are good. What is new with you?"

"Well, my friend Lily passed away." I had told her all about Lily on our weekend together.

"I'm so sorry. I know how much she meant to you. Had she been sick?"

"Yeah, but she kept it from me. So, it came as a shock."

We talk about what's been going on with each other since we last spoke a few months ago. Then I say, "I'm working on something to honor her. Actually, I want to create a community like yours."

"Wow. How would you do that?"

"She left some land that would be perfect for it. I hope to talk to Julian and ask him some questions."

"You know that is a major undertaking."

I laugh. "Yes, I do know that. I'm just exploring the possibility."

"Sorry," she says, "I just remember how long it took. But, I will have him call you."

"That would be great. I'm sorry I didn't get a chance to stop and see you." I didn't want to interrupt her summer plans.

"Me too," she says with a hint of sadness.

She tells me about her summer, and I talk about my Camino.

"I'm glad we're still friends," I say.

The next day Julian calls. I pepper him with questions, taking notes the whole time. He gives me the names of two others in the intentional community world. Over the coming days, I talk to them, and they e-mail me things they think may be helpful.

I create a portfolio that explains my grand plan.

An entire month passes.

Finally, I feel relief.

I meet with Steven when I get back. I lay out my vision, my mission.

"I had no idea what you were thinking. This is interesting," he says. "But this is a massive project. The money from Lily wouldn't come close to covering it."

"Understood. But I think it would be great. The plans here are based on Lily's parcel of land."

"Wow, you did your research. And you've visited a community like this?"

"Yeah. I loved it. Happy people."

"Let me review this and make a few calls. We can meet up for a drink next week."

"Perfect," I respond. We shake hands.

I walk from Steven's office, slightly less confident about my big plan.

Over drinks the next week, Steven says, "I've gotten some good feedback, and a few possible investors. But we'll likely need to go into this together to get enough backing."

"Absolutely," I say. "But I don't want you to put yourself at risk."

"It's more my name, but we would still be partners."

"Whatever you think is best. I'm fine with anything."

I resume walking Vita and Finn, though I'm no longer their full-time dog walker; I've been replaced. I meet up with Jimmy often. I share meals with Mary, Ben, Steven, his family, or any combination at least once a week. I visit my mom and my brothers, though, I now consider Madison home.

I've been reading more than writing—mostly cohousing and community-based books.

Over dinner with his family, Steven says, "I like the line, 'Live a life you don't want to escape from'."

Lauren thinks the project "unique."

I bring up possible names for the community. Awaken? or A New Day?

"Maybe a little too new age," Emily offers.

"I've been saving this for tonight," Steven says with a smirk. "We've gotten more than enough interest. The funding will no longer be an issue." Then adds, "Ben's in too."

"I can't believe it," I say excitedly. "That's fantastic."

Lily's money and the land are the guarantee, but most residents that come, will buy in, owning their home. We just need to find people who share the vision.

"I love the idea of this place, Jack," Emily says. "As a family, we're still discussing the possibilities."

I say, stealing a line, "If we build it, they will come."

Months pass. Before winter turns to Spring, we finally get the green light.

I buy a small teardrop camper. It is just big enough for a full bed inside and an outdoor kitchen that opens in the back. It is perfect to pull behind my trusty Subaru. Their colors even match.

Covid hits.

Everything stops.

Sitting alone in Lily's place, I often connect with the many people whose paths I've crossed. I'm grateful now for having exchanged contact information with so many from my travels. FaceTime and Zoom calls help with the loneliness. I also read, write, and play the guitar to pass the days. Eventually, I go back and forth between Lily's and my mom's.

Time drags as the plans for the community remain on hold. But seeing what's happening in the world, I feel nothing but gratitude for my friends and family staying safe.

By summer, we break ground, but progress is slow. I am not the general contractor, but I am on site most days and many nights.

The earth is moved, the road in is paved, utilities come, and geothermal is laid. My excitement builds with each new day.

Almost five months after our delayed start, I'm on the property, camping alone. It's a beautiful fall day. I walk the land, climbing over rolling hills, planning where paths will go. When the sun goes down, the temperature falls. I sit on a deck I've constructed; it surrounds a large fire pit, and has benches built in. I look up to a cloudless sky, a full moon shines down—so bright, I don't need a flashlight.

I smile, thinking of Lily and her dream of someday living on this land. I know she'd approve of what this land, and I, are becoming. I remember her saying, "Become your best self."

Out loud, I say, "I'm working on it each day."

My line in her eulogy about her being the wind in my sails is true; I would not have become the man I am today without her pushing me. I would have remained adrift at sea. She gave me the wind, but I was at the tiller, steering my own course.

I'm excited to be here. I've got a home to create.

It will be quite a journey ahead, building this, to be sure.

I have moments where I question this unconventional plan. It's a risk, I know. I'm betting with house money, Lily's money. It's her legacy that's at stake. The payoff won't be riches, it will be a lasting community.

I hope Ben was right when he told me, "You can help others see something they couldn't see before."

The calendar keeps turning. Progress continues while another winter passes.

It is a beautiful spring night with many gathered here on the land, camping out. Most of Lily's circle, a dozen potential residents, and my family and friends. Many are wearing shirts fresh off the silkscreen, our logo centered. A sun rising from behind the largest hill, our community centered in front, then the words Harmony Hill Cohousing, in a subtle lower-case font.

Several of us walk through fields of green. The footpaths are already well-worn. I think back to my dreams in the past, specifically of Vanlife. How much simpler it would be to wander aimlessly, but I smile, knowing now, that life to be so incomplete—alone, with no real community. We circle the site as the sun sets. No permanent structures have been completed yet. We have a port-a-potty, running water, and a couple of light poles up, plus two more teardrop campers and two large platform tents. Our little camping village arcs around the fire at the back of the site. Through the flames I see some of the equipment used to build this place; a backhoe, a bulldozer, both at rest for the next two days.

We sit sipping cocoa or beer, discussing a life here filled with more nights like this; gathering to talk and share. It reminds me of evenings camping in the Northwoods when I was a kid. We tell stories and laugh until sleep begins to call.

In the morning, we walk through the site, the foundations all poured.

"I love the simple lines on the Common House, and almost identical details on the living spaces," Sophie says, as a group of us walk along rough gravel paths.

"I do too. I helped design it." I smirk.

"I like the light wood. It's different," one of the new faces says. "And I love the blue accents. It reminds me of a wave."

"Serene was the feeling it's intended to evoke."

"I like that the paths gently flow from one space to the next," my mom says.

"That's all Lauren," I say, nodding towards her. "She's the landscape architect."

"Well, almost—and this is my first job."

We all gather around two large tables and enjoy a tasty lunch. My brother Jamie cooked the hamburgers on the grill, and Mary made a delicious salad. After we're nourished, everyone gets to work.

Most of our efforts are focused in the "Common House:" painting, laying flooring, installing fixtures, hanging doors—the G.C. (General Contractor) left us a list. We are all just a set of extra hands, but many of us have progressed our skills as this place comes to be.

At dinner, I say to those gathered, "Thanks for your help this weekend, and over the last year. It's been amazing, together helping build this place once called 'unique'."

I glance at Lauren and smile. She nods.

"Steven here," I say, looking at him, "he's been with me since day one. Now he's up here almost every day." Steven brought in a new partner to his firm so he could focus on this project. "We wouldn't be here without him. He's doing the behind-the-scenes work, the hard stuff, as well as getting dirty."

"But this is your vision, Jack," he says. "Lily believed in you. She would be proud."

"She did, surprisingly, long before I did myself."

Lily helped me take myself seriously, treating me with a respect I didn't feel I deserved. Lucky for me, she was looking—then saw *something* in me.

And, when you want something, all the universe conspires in helping you achieve it."

Paulo Coelho, *The Alchemist*

TWENTY-FOUR / build

April 13 –   Cross Plains, Wisconsin

"Can you hand me the nail gun," Randy says, from halfway up a ladder.

"Here you go," I say with a smile. "I'm gonna go check on the others."

I walk out of the two-bedroom unit and around the corner to one of the two one-bedrooms in this residential structure.

"Hey, Tom. How's it going?" He's about to cut a piece of hardwood flooring.

"Good, but I'll need more soon."

"I'll have Patrick bring some over."

Tom and Randy are married and have a little girl, Mylah, who's four. Tom is an artist and stays at home with her, while Randy teaches at the same small college where Lily taught. I love these guys, they're friendly and hardworking. They were some of the first to start attending our monthly informational meetings.

These get-togethers started early on. We started posting on various cohousing blogs and put out flyers around Madison and the surrounding towns; gauging interest in our concept before we even got the go ahead. Our first few meetings were at Lily's place, but we moved to larger venues as interest picked up. We had a core group of about fifteen before breaking ground.

As I'm walking towards the Common House, I slow down and say, "Hey, ladies," as I pass Lauren and a couple of her friends working on the landscaping.

One of them asks, "Jack, what's for lunch?"

"Tacos, I think. Mary's on lunch duty today."

Our community has grown larger over the last few months. We now have forty-four residents. That includes Steven's family, my mom and brothers (though Pat will be away at college down at U of I), Mary, and one of her friends. Sophie, her husband, and daughter are still a maybe. We have a single mom with twin boys, a few retired couples, and a few senior folks who currently live alone. Families, though, are the bulk; the largest has three kids. All in all, it's a perfect mix. That was the hope all along. Our kids, sixteen in all, range in age from two to eighteen. Though one couple is expecting their first before move-in day.

We have eight residential structures with a total of twenty-six living units, and a maximum occupancy of sixty full time residents. The housing units range from a studio (1-2 residents), one bedroom (1-2), two bedroom (2-4), two bedroom with a loft (up to 5). I will be in a two-bedroom, a violation of our rules, but a community vote approved my exception.

There are a few rules, each agreed upon by our members. Most were easy and we had a consensus. In my example we have guidelines for the number of residents for each kind of unit. Me being single should have kept me in a one-bedroom, but I pled my case to the community, saying I wouldn't be single forever. Luckily for me, everyone agreed. But there have been instances where it came down to a vote. An example of that: should we have guest suites in the Common House? Both sides were heard, and a cheaper, more communal option was chosen.

Steven and his family decided to move in once others joined. Emily and their daughters were hesitant but started to see the benefits after meeting those coming on board. They will be in one of the two bedrooms with a loft. My mom and brothers are in a two-bedroom. Though my favorite space is the studio, one single open space with a small bathroom attached. There's a Murphy Bed built in, which when closed, becomes a desk. One of our retired residents is a woodworking ace; he built these beds from scratch.

I said before that most units will be owned by those moving in, but several units will be available for rent, including for those who wish to test out our communal life.

I walk up five stairs to a broad, wrap-around covered porch and through full glass double doors, to the only complete space — our Common House. It's still not a hundred percent, but the kitchen and bathrooms work. The bunk room upstairs called 'The Albergue', now sleeps up to twelve. Our camping village is still here, though the port-a-potty is gone.

"Hi, Mary," I say, "it looks great." The counter from the kitchen, which opens to the huge dining space, is laid out with a delicious-looking spread. Platters filled with various kinds of meat, beans, veggies, salsas, and hard and soft shells are all lined up.

"I'm about to ring the bell," she says, smiling.

"Great, call them in."

Soon, the twenty or so on site today are sitting in the dining hall. We talk while we scarf down a well-earned lunch. In the background, a playlist of seventies songs plays on a portable speaker.

Tom says something which I know to be true. "I think for all of us it feels special to be building this community from the ground up, and watching it grow."

A few voices express their agreement.

"You're right," I say, "and building it together is key."

When we finish eating, five youngsters head back outside to play with Emily and Alyssa. Alyssa, now a junior in high school.

Our work continues until late in the afternoon when our guests start to arrive. Friends and family of some members, curious where their loved ones will be living, are coming up to see the place and enjoy a meal together. After dinner, I take them on a tour. It starts here.

"This is the dining hall," I say, "which seats sixty to eat, obviously more without the tables, and maybe twenty or so for an early morning yoga class that a few of our residents will be organizing."

I lead them to an almost empty room, just off the dining hall. There are blocks, Legos and a dollhouse on the floor now. "This is the 'KidSpace' where a small daycare will be set up," I say. "Stay-at-home parents, and our retirees, can volunteer to interact with the little ones."

"This next room is my favorite," I say as we move down a wide hallway. "This is 'Lily's Place,' the largest of the rooms downstairs. It will be the music room, and probably a hangout for the younger crowd." Most of the residents moving here never knew Lily but I wanted to make sure her memory and legacy live on. I hope to incorporate her in more ways as this place continues to grow. For now, her place here is enough.

"The last room down here is the 'Artist's Retreat,'" I say. "Our residents will be bringing their favorite things to donate to the community. So far, we have a pottery wheel, kiln, loom, and painting supplies lined up to be in here. Across the hall we have three small bathrooms, each with a toilet and sink."

"Let's head upstairs."

Everyone follows me into the bunk room.

"This is where most of you will be sleeping tonight. It's nothing special, but a place to rest your head. Across the hall is a large bath with a couple of showers. It's unisex, so don't be surprised."

"We also have two large multipurpose rooms up here, but we don't have any specific plans for these yet."

My life the last few years led me to new places, and I experienced many new things. Those I found useful, I incorporated into my original plan. Luckily, most made it through the several design evolutions. Now, everywhere we go, reminds me of a place in my past. This community is a collection of lessons I have learned.

We head back down and enter the kitchen.

"A few of our residents recommended these appliances. It's all commercial grade. There wasn't much pushback, since we will be cooking for up to sixty people at least once a week." There is a huge side-by-side fridge with see-through doors, a separate freezer, a six-burner stove with griddle, a massive sink, and open stainless-steel shelving on one wall, filled with plates, bowls, and cups.

"No dishwasher?" One of the guests asks.

"Nope. As a group, we decided that washing dishes would be another communal activity," I say. "I had shared a story of a night on the Camino de Santiago where forty pilgrims were dining together at an albergue. After the meal, four large buckets of water were brought out, two soapy, two not. Like in an assembly line every dish and glass were washed and dried in ten minutes. It was fun."

"How big are the kitchens in the homes?" another asks.

"We'll go in each size unit, so you'll see them."

We head down another wide hallway. I slide open a barn-style door, to an empty room and say "This will be the laundry room, with three commercial-grade washers and three dryers. Having this will free up space in each unit, though some residents are putting stackable washer/dryers in one of their closets. Each unit, except for the studios, will be plumbed for that possibility. But I pushed for this space; it will be another potential meeting point; to bring about spontaneous interactions between residents. At least that's the idea."

"Our next stop isn't really a room. It's more of a coffee nook," I say, standing next to the laundry room, in an area recessed about eight feet. "One of our residents is donating a high-end expresso machine. It will be in here along with two or three small tables. It's another meeting point. One of our members is painting a beautiful sign to hang here. We're going to call this area 'Good Decisions'."

"That's an unusual name," someone says.

"I guess," I say, "but it's a simple reminder that the quality of our lives depends solely on the quality of our decisions."

I lead the group out the side door, to the wrap-around porch, then to the paved patio. There no steps here, so the main floor is handicap accessible.

"Let's go around back. I'll show you the woodworking shop."

On the way, I point out where the dog park will be, and then the "solar patch" at the base of a hill. "Every building has panels, too." Behind the Common House is a compact wooden building, "This was constructed completely by us," I say proudly. "Two of our residents have large shops in their current homes and have slowly started bringing the best equipment they have up here to share. Not only their tools, but also their knowledge. You'll get to see some of their work on our tour."

Together, we walk over to the housing area. The buildings are close together, separated by a wide concrete walkway that runs the length of this area, there are four structures on each side. A narrower path, paved with stones, circles each of the buildings.

"Is the layout of each one bedroom the same?" someone asks.

"No. There are two variations for both the one and two bedrooms. Some units are two levels, but most are on one. We wanted different options, but the square footage is almost the same for each type."

When we're in a two-bedroom, someone says, "It would be hard to have family here for a large Thanksgiving meal."

"You're right," I say with a smile. "There are tradeoffs to be sure. If someone is considering moving here from a bigger house, they'll need to weigh what's most important. This community, a life here, is not for everyone."

Opinions vary, and that's okay. I know if I was visiting us, and it was my first time seeing a cohousing community, I would think it not necessarily ideal. I understand how some people may react without knowing what life here is meant to be.

"I don't know where I would put everything," the same woman says.

"I get that," I say. "I know people have lots of stuff. I never had a lot personally, but many in our community are downsizing and simplifying for the first time. They say it's liberating."

Then I add, "I find having fewer desires and fewer possessions makes my life happier. I'm more content."

"To each his own," my antagonist says.

"On that we agree," I say with a smile, or maybe it's a smirk. Then I add, "Another cool thing, not everyone needs to have one of everything. We will have over twenty families here, and if they lived in their own house, they'd need more stuff; lawn equipment is a good example, here, not everyone needs their own lawnmower or rake. Plus, we don't need garages for storage; we have a temporary shelter to store bikes, maintenance equipment, and the like. We *will* be building a barn in the next year or so to take its place."

As we are walking to see a one-bedroom unit, I say, "When I was a kid, we had a huge closet filled with games. Here, we will be using the library concept for games, books, and even seldom used kitchen appliances; so, each unit will not need to store one of everything. So, we will have one game of Monopoly that can be used by anyone. Plus, you should be able to find someone to join your game. There's talk of a weekly game night in the Common House."

"What about video games?" A teenager asks.

"In your unit, sure, just be aware of the volume. We've used soundproof insulation between each unit, but it hasn't been put to the test yet. In the Common House, the agreed to rule, was no video games, but that may change before we open. If it changes, headphones will be required."

"Maybe the empty room by 'The Albergue' could be the gaming room," he says.

I give him a broad smile, "We hadn't thought of that. That's a great idea."

"Our last stop is what we're calling the Studio Building. There are eight living units, all small studios, four on each level," I say as we walk into one that's finished. It's a tight fit with so many of us in less than five hundred square feet.

"Make sure you see the bathroom," I say. "I saw something similar in Finland."

"It's small, and there's no shower curtain. It all gets wet, but it's easy to get used to. Plus, it's super easy to clean."

We head back to the Common House where a campfire is blazing. Some guests will head back home, but the majority are staying the night.

Our residents walk their friends and family to the parking lot, twenty-five yards from the living spaces; cars are not allowed any closer. Those staying return with their sleeping bags and packs.

About thirty of us are gathered around the fire, talking, when one of our guests introduces us to the best S'more I've ever tasted. She has brought several bags of Keebler Fudge Striped cookies. She gives each of us a long wooden skewer, and we all toast a marshmallow, then sandwich it between two of the cookies. Yum!

The next day, we work for a couple of hours, then it's play time. It's Sunday Funday after all. Games of Bocce, Bags (also known as Cornhole), and volleyball are played. Eventually the crowd starts to peel away.

My mom, brothers and I are the last to leave.

They help me close up. Lights out, doors locked.

We walk down a gentle slope to our cars.

"I cannot believe you actually pulled this off," Patrick says. "I thought you were crazy when you first showed us your plans."

"To be honest, I'm as surprised as you."

Patrick hugs each of us, then tosses his pack in the back of the Subaru.

"I love you guys," he says with a smile. Then heads south to Champaign.

Mom hugs me and says, "I'm proud of you, Jack. Your dad would be too."

"Thanks mom. I know you *both* are," I say smiling, "I love you."

I hug Jamie and say, "Thanks for your help."

"It was fun," he says, "I can't wait to move in."

He and mom head back home.

I jump in my company vehicle, an orange Toyota Tacoma with our logo stenciled on the doors, and head to Lily's house, which I still call home.

TWENTY-FIVE / place

August 18 –   Harmony Hill Cohousing

It's not officially move in day yet, but the place is complete. The overall aesthetic came out just as intended, and the quality of the construction is even better than I imagined. The landscaping looks amazing, splashes of color are already scattered about. A good number of us moved up about a week ago, but it's just a dozen of us here on the weekdays.

This afternoon, a few are gathered in Lily's Place talking. It's cozy in here with two oversized leather couches, and a few chairs, all of which have been donated. Steven is here, so is Lauren, Tom, Randy, and one of our newest members, Dr. DeVries, who has long been retired. Surprise … Nathalie and Julian are here too. I invited them months ago, but they wanted to wait until it was finished.

Steven and I are meeting with a reporter from the *Wisconsin State Journal*, who plans to do a story on our community. The reporter is a friend of our resident doctor.

I'm sitting next to Nathalie, who has been here the last few days. Our time together scares me a bit; my feelings for her are back and even more intense. She said she feels the same, and that "our connection runs deep." She and Julian are only here for two short weeks.

I picked Julian and her up from the airport and we spent the first two days in Madison at Lily's house, not yet on the market. We explored the town and campus before Julian took off on his own. Nathalie and I went hiking and sailing. It was a blast. We went furniture shopping. I asked for her help choosing things for the common spaces, as well as my place.

Before the reporter shows up, Steven pulls me aside. "You take the lead when he arrives. This place comes from your imagination. It's your vision. You are the face of Harmony."

"I appreciate that, but it's about the community," I say. "And we're partners in this."

"I know Jack, but trust me, you make it a better story."

Before my life changed, I would have deferred. Insisting someone else take the lead. But my demeanor and confidence has started to grow. Even my public speaking has come a long way, starting with Lily's eulogy. Since then, a few book readings and short talks about Harmony Hill have helped me quiet some of those nerves. I'm still learning and growing, unsure what might be ahead.

Right on time, the reporter pulls into our paved parking lot. Dr. Devries, Steven, and I walk up to greet him.

"Good afternoon, Bob," the good doctor says.

"Hi, Jerry," he says. "Great to see you. It's been a few years."

"It has been a while. I'm glad you think we may be worthy of a story."

"I'm Jack," I say, reaching out my hand.

"Steven." The last two shake hands.

We head back and share greetings with those we pass.

Nathalie winks, and mouths "good luck."

We give Bob the well-practiced tour—he seems impressed.

Then we head to Lily's Place to answer his questions. Dr. Devries peels away.

We explain the concept of cohousing, and its origins.

"A little like the communes in the seventies," Bob says.

"We're a little more refined." I smile.

I talk about my travels and the inspiration for this place.

He looks up from his notepad.

"Did you write that book?" he asks, surprised.

"Yeah, I did."

"I am the one who wrote the review," he says. "I loved it. I've given copies to my nieces and nephews, and one even followed your lead. She spent two months walking in Italy."

"Wow. I love that story." It feels good to have inspired somebody.

He asks about the funding to get this built.

"I was given a substantial sum a few years ago by a friend of ours. So that helped. But Steven and a couple of other friends, *with means,* helped make it all possible. Together we formed the corporation, "Lily's Trust.""

"So, the company that operates the totality of the place is owned by your investors?" And the residents own their space and a share of the common areas?"

"You're the guy when it comes to that," I say looking at Steven.

He nods and smirks at me.

"Basically, but with a few kinks," he says. "Cohousing is designed to be a place people stay for the long term. There are stipulations; an example would be, if someone moves, or passes away, a set price will be paid, factoring in preset adjustments which likely will be well below the market value. The unit will go back to the community. The next resident will likely pay more, and any excess will go into the trust to help cover costs for improvements and maintenance, or whatever else the community decides."

"How do you decide what to do with the excess funds?"

"We try and work towards a consensus, but things often come down to a vote."

"Do the investors—say you two—do you have more say?"

"No, we're all only one vote, and that's per unit, not resident," I say.

"Why is that?"

"We don't want any family to have more power than another."

"Does your company expect to make a profit? The investors?"

"Everything put into the corporation to get this going earns six percent. This was not intended to be a big money-making venture," Steven says.

"How does someone get a mortgage for a property here?"

I chime in. "Since we haven't found a bank willing to lend here, another corporation, one that we own together, operates solely to fund the purchase of property at Harmony Hill."

"Are all the units resident owned?"

"Not all. We keep some as rental units. We want about twenty percent of our residents to be able to rent, those that don't have cash saved. All these tenants will be on three-month leases, which ideally, will be renewed indefinitely."

"Are there H.O.A. fees, or what would be comparable in cohousing?"

"Yes, but with everyone pitching in to help maintain things, it's really not that much."

"With your solar farm, are you going to be self-sustaining?"

"Hopefully, but we're not sure," I say. "We have geothermal for heating and cooling. But we may add a turbine if the solar isn't enough."

"You're in this for the long term then." he says with a nod. Then he asks, "So, Steven, how did you get involved with this project?"

"Well, when Jack came to me with his plan, I was skeptical," he says, looking at me. "It took me some time to understand what it was all about, and even longer for my wife and kids. But, once I realized it made sense financially, I was on board to at least help Jack get it started. To be honest, starting the company was refreshing for me. I was happy to be involved with something so different, after twenty-five years of doing the same thing."

I look at Steven and smile. I knew he thought it was crazy at first, but I didn't know he felt renewed by his involvement.

"Then once we started meeting those that would be joining the community, it didn't take us long to decide."

"Can you describe the typical person that moves into cohousing?"

"There is no typical, I don't think," I say. "From my experience, it's people of any age, any sex or sexuality, all races, single people, couples, families, retirees. And that's what we want, a mix of everything."

Steven adds, "The people that are drawn to this type of life—seem to me to like being with people, are friendly, hardworking and authentic."

"Can anyone move here?"

"No. A person or family must apply," I say. "Going forward, those buying in will be required to rent the unit they intend to buy for three months, and then decide if we fit. This is for both them and the community."

Steven says, "This is a new venture, so none of this has been tested. Those in the community, and we're at fifty-four, all gathered over the last year or so and have become like an extended family. If anyone felt out of place, they could simply drop out. That hasn't happened."

"It's a beautiful day," I say to Bob. "Would you like to take a stroll along our walking path?"

"Sure. I'm in no hurry to get back to the office."

"Steven, do you want to come?" I ask.

"You two go ahead. I have a few things I need to get done."

We cross the mowed field, then past our large fenced in garden and compost heap and join with a path covered in wood chips.

Bob asks more about my travels, and how I met Lily. He asks about my family and growing up with a single mom.

I am taken aback when he says, "single mom," questioning how he would know that. Then I remember he'd read my book.

"Do you think that played a part in your quest to create this place?"

"Of course," I say. "That was a big one. I think if we'd lived in a community like this when my dad died, our family would have had the support needed to better help us heal. Another big thing was Lily. After her husband died, she kept to herself, and struggled to ask for the help she needed. She too, would have benefited from a life in cohousing."

"I am starting to understand the appeal."

We take the shorter loop and head back.

We find Steven and Dr. Devries in the Common House. The four of us head back outside.

"I enjoyed my visit. I appreciate your time. I think I have what I need."

We walk Bob to his car.

He turns back and looks at the place. "Impressive."

I look back too. Our little community centered perfectly on the lush green hill rising from behind. I chuckle to myself, knowing that wasn't planned. I also love the gravel path that meanders from the parking lot to the large courtyard. The path is now flanked by fifteen-foot evergreens, freshly planted.

I think his visit went well. I wonder what he might write.

Three days later Nathalie and I are in Grand Teton National Park. We are on a road trip, so I can show her some of the beauty here in the States.

We head into the canyon behind Jenny Lake and hike for hours. Our path cuts through trees alongside a river; its flow slows the higher we climb. We are headed to an aptly named body of water, Lake Solitude. We arrive exhausted. After a few minutes to catch our breath, we strip down to our underwear and jump into the lake. It's so cold, it stings. The mountains surround us on all sides. It's a stunningly beautiful place. We lay out on huge boulders and dry off in the sun.

"I'm impressed," Nathalie tells me. "It's more beautiful than anything I've seen in Belgium."

"I know, I was here a few years ago and wanted to come back," I say. "I'm glad it's with you."

She smiles.

"Last week, Steven and I were talking about you and me. He knows I really like you, but knows we've decided to be *just* friends. He told me about a line from some movie, like, 'When you're young, you think you'll *truly* connect with so many people. But, when you're older, you realize it only happens a few times in one's life'."

Nathalie cranes her neck and looks me in the eyes, and says, "I know this."

I stare into her eyes.
Time stops.
I kiss her.
It is decided.

Over our last few days together, we paint what our near future holds in broad strokes. My situation is flexible now that Harmony is up and running. Nathalie is living on her own, in an apartment near Bruges, and teaching. Our plan is simple; at least a long weekend together every three weeks.

After Nathalie returns home, I think about why she and I feel such a bond. We met knowing only how each other looked. Our conversation that first night flowed easily. We opened up to each other quickly. I liked that she is so genuine. Maybe it's the fact there were no expectations early on. We were ourselves; there was no pretending. As this is my first serious relationship, maybe I don't know what romantic love is. But I haven't felt *this* before. No one in high school, or college, no one in Madison, not along my treks. Never *this*. Nothing. Even. Close.

TWENTY-SIX / home

August 26 (the following year) –   Harmony Hill Cohousing

The crowd spills onto the deck and patio. Steven and I squirm our way into the Common House, as *Jessie's Girl* plays over the sound system. Jamie and Alyssa are the DJ's tonight. The dining hall is decorated with an "Eighties" theme for tonight's celebration. It has been one year since our official opening. We even have a large event tent set up on the soccer field for later.

I give Nathalie a quick hug as I walk by. It was a long road, but ultimately, she landed a teaching job and a green card. I'm so happy she's here.

I step onto 'the soapbox' and say in a loud voice, "Thank you all for being here. I'm glad everyone could make the time to celebrate together."

The room is still kind of loud, but the crowd shushes itself.

"Alyssa," I say, "would you like to unveil your latest project?"

She and Lauren are standing beneath a long piece of fabric, hanging high on a wall.

"I painted this in honor of Lily," she says. The sisters yank down.

"Home isn't a place, but a feeling" is painted in a beautiful cursive font. Surrounding the words: trees, vines, flowers, butterflies, and bees. This is the first time I've seen it completed. It's amazing.

The crowd gasps, and then starts to applaud. Alyssa smiles and takes a bow.

Once the crowd settles, I say, "The seed for Harmony was planted five years ago at the Colectivo. It is where I met Lily, the one who made this all possible." I look at the crowd and think about that day. "It was her dream to one day live on this land; and in a way, she is." I pause for a second. "I want to share one of my new favorite things—it's when I hear one of our kids say to another, "Let's meet at Lily's Place." It melts my heart every time." I pause again. "I know it took some time for us to get into a rhythm, but I hope everyone is enjoying our life here, as much as I am."

The crowd gives its approval.

"Okay," I say. "I would also like to introduce our 58th official member, my friend Nathalie."

The crowd cheers, and the place gets loud.

Nathalie gives a wave, and with a raised voice, says, "It is wonderful to be here with all of you."

"And since she's living with me, my unit is now in compliance," I joke, at least to myself.

"I also want you all to meet some of my friends here tonight."

"I'll introduce you," I say, looking around the room, "and if you each could give a wave."

First Johannes and Emilia. Julian and his wife. Then Bruno, my friend from the Via Francigena. Mario and Anne. Brody and his new wife, Megan. Jimmy. And I am most pleased that Lina, yes *that* Lina, is here too.

I look around the room at the many photos hanging on the walls. All of them, groups of people in the community, together. My favorite though, Lily's picture hanging in 'her place.' It's the photo that stood beside her casket, beautiful in her middle years, staring into the void. Another smaller picture of our circle on that night of celebration hangs nearby.

"I also want to thank everyone for their help with the construction of our picnic shelter. It's finally complete. The fireplace will be perfect to huddle around on the chillier and wetter days. And by next year, we should have our barn. It seems the sauna will keep getting pushed back," I complain jokingly.

"Over the last year, I have thought a lot about the birth of this place. What led to its creation? I've looked back at my life, connecting ... it was Steve Jobs who said, 'You can't connect the dots looking forward; you can only connect them looking backwards'. He's right. I could not have planned a path to get here. The stars simply aligned and led us all here tonight."

"I've been thinking about that as I work on my next book, and FYI, you'll all be in it. It's about the building of this place, and our community. I'm calling it *Life Reimagined*. The goal of *this* book is to educate."

"What was the goal of your first book?" Someone asks.

"To inspire readers to travel, to think, and get outside their comfort zone. Hopefully, it shows there are options in life."

"Enjoy the party," I say as I step off the soapbox. I wade through the crowd, looking for Nathalie.

Tonight, is the first time most of my old friends will meet her. Together, we make the rounds.

When we run across Brody, he and I introduce our partners, who start to chat. Then he says to me, "So, what's next for you?"

"My focus now is to help others find community. It's my driving force—trying to connect people in a real way. I think it's something that many people are missing."

"That's great," he says. "We are just *now* starting to find a circle of friends, and I been there five years already."

We stop and talk to Lina. She and Nathalie have become good friends over the last year. I told Nathalie everything that happened with Lina when we spoke after Lily's passing. She is the only person I talked to about how I acted that night. I felt as if a weight was being lifted as we spoke.

Then, Nathalie and I locate Jimmy who is sporting a well-trimmed beard. He's talking to Lauren, who, it turns out, was in one of his classes Junior year. The four of us talk about tonight's festivities. Later, I tell Nathalie that Jimmy and I are going to take a walk. I have only seen him a couple times in the past year and want to catch up.

He and I head through a patch of newly planted trees, then onto the path that winds its way to the top of the hill. He tells me about his life in Milwaukee, and how much he likes his job. Then he says, "I've finally been able to do some traveling."

"Awesome," I say.

"I might even be taking a gap year, probably next year."

"What!" I exclaim, my smile growing. "I think that's great. Do it!"

We make it to the top of the hill. I look down on what I've helped create. I smile and shake my head.

"How about you?" he asks. "Any upcoming travel plans?"

"We're headed to Belgium over her winter break," I say. "And I'm going to Colorado Springs next month. I'm meeting with a group and looking at some land for a potential community. Then Brody and I are going backpacking."

"Sweet," he says. Then adds, "I'm starting to rethink my priorities. It feels good." He looks at me and smiles wide.

This is the happiest I've ever seen him. I feel grateful that I could return the favor … knowing I've played a part.

A while later, the party moves to the tent. Nathalie and I join the crowd on the dance floor. We dance together for a handful of songs, including a slow one, before we head outside to the fire. We sit on a bench with glasses of wine.

Later, the flames grow as we start a bonfire out near the soccer field.

The sky is crystal clear, the Milky Way visible, here, miles away from anything else. Kids are running around and laughing. Conversations are had. Feelings are felt.

Later, I play the song, *Tears in Heaven*, on the guitar.

After I finish, Brody takes the guitar, a surprise, and plays, *Three Little Birds,* singing along.

"You inspired me," he says with his cheesy grin.

The party continues into the night. Eventually, the crowd starts to dwindle, but many of us stand arm in arm around the fire. We sing a handful of my favorite camp songs—ones I've shared.

As a song ends, I tug on the back of Nathalie's sweatshirt.

Slowly, we back away, then turn.

Walking hand in hand.

I look up—all the stars are out tonight.

These dots, these choices, yet to be made.

I live life, connecting.

My life, my constellation.

The vastness, the options.

The choice, mine.

.

.

I find myself here.

Now.

In this *moment*, along *my* journey.

.

And, in *her* journey, too.

~ A Farewell for Now ~

I've thought a lot about what's led me here. The best way I can describe it would be to list the things I have been lucky enough to practice over these past few years.

- Smile. Just smile.
- Eliminate distractions. Then use the time you dedicated to - scrolling, streaming, or gaming - to do something productive. Books. Writing. Thinking.
- *Enjoy* the process of becoming who you will be tomorrow. Good habits. Trial and error. Find a creative outlet. Trust me, eventually self-confidence will follow.
- Find solitude. Go in, think, and dig deep.
- Listen—to you. You gotta be you. To live a good life, you need to live a life that represents you. Without knowing what makes you "unique," you won't know what activities to pursue.
- Simplify. It's not hard, but you must decide.
- Travel (if you can). Prioritize. Travel to open your mind, and to learn the lessons it will teach. Travel to find joy. Travel doesn't always mean leaving home—but finding home—your place—inside yourself. AND, if you can, take a long, long walk.
- Be a creator. It's freeing to let your inner artist out.
- Find your others. If you don't think anyone is out there like you — you haven't looked. There are pockets of consciousness everywhere.
- Discover your passion. To find it, you must "do the work."

All of this, in hopes that … to paraphrase Nietzsche — "You find what has mastered your soul, and at the same time blessed it. This is where you find your true self."

I have found that without a dream, life is mundane. My dream *now* is simple: a continued life with others. My wife to be … and kids. Limited wants and limited needs. And to share our concept of community.

I will continue writing. I hope you will continue reading.

Enjoy your journey!

~ Jack Dufour

ABOUT THE AUTHOR

Michael Burnett was born and raised outside of Chicago. He spent most of his life in the Midwest before a move later in life to Portland, Oregon. There his love for being outdoors in nature grew, as did his passion for hiking. His evolution to a writer was slow. It wasn't until he escaped a nine-to-five life and started living a life filled with adventure that he put pen to paper.

Michael is a father of two grown children and is back living in the Chicago area, where he enjoys spending time with his four grandkids. When he's not traveling, Michael can be found enjoying time outdoors or planning his next adventure with his significant other. They are now making plans for their next long walk.

For more information about Michael and his current project, visit his website: walkingandwriting.com. You can also follow Michael on Instagram @seekingclaritywhilewalking

If you enjoyed this book, please leave a review on Amazon.com. Thanks!

ALSO AVAILABLE FROM

Michael Burnett's travel memoir, *Finding Myself Along the Way*, follows his five-hundred-mile walk along the Camino de Santiago. His story starts upon his arrival in the French city of Saint-Jean-Pied-du-Port and is a day-by-day account of his month-long walk across Spain. In his novel, *Lost Myself for a Minute*, this section of the Camino is covered in three pages; in his memoir, it is the whole book. It was this journey that led the author to his passion for writing. This is a story about one man who reaches the middle of his life and asks the question ... Is this all there is?

After finding the courage to upend a life of convention and security, the author leaves literally everything behind. At age fifty, he embarks on a voyage of self-discovery and adventure in his search to uncover what his life can be. In this book, he shares with the reader the path that led him to walk this ancient pilgrimage to Santiago de Compostela. You'll meet the many people he encounters and learn how his connections with fellow pilgrims allow him to open up, both with others and himself. Along the way, the reader will come to understand how a journey on the Camino gives a new perspective, as well as teaches many lessons about life, hope, and resilience.

COMING IN LATE 2023: *Coming Into Focus* is Michael Burnett's follow up to his novel, *Lost Myself for a Minute*. Follow Jack as he continues to strive to becomes the man he hopes to be. Many of the same characters from *Lost Myself for a Minute* are back, along with a few new faces, as Jack transforms yet again. He continues his travels, but he is no longer a solo traveler. He and his life partner will circle the globe in their quest to find the answers to life's big questions.

If you liked *Lost Myself for a Minute*, you'll love this story of love, loss, and the search for meaning.